DISNEY
PRINCESS

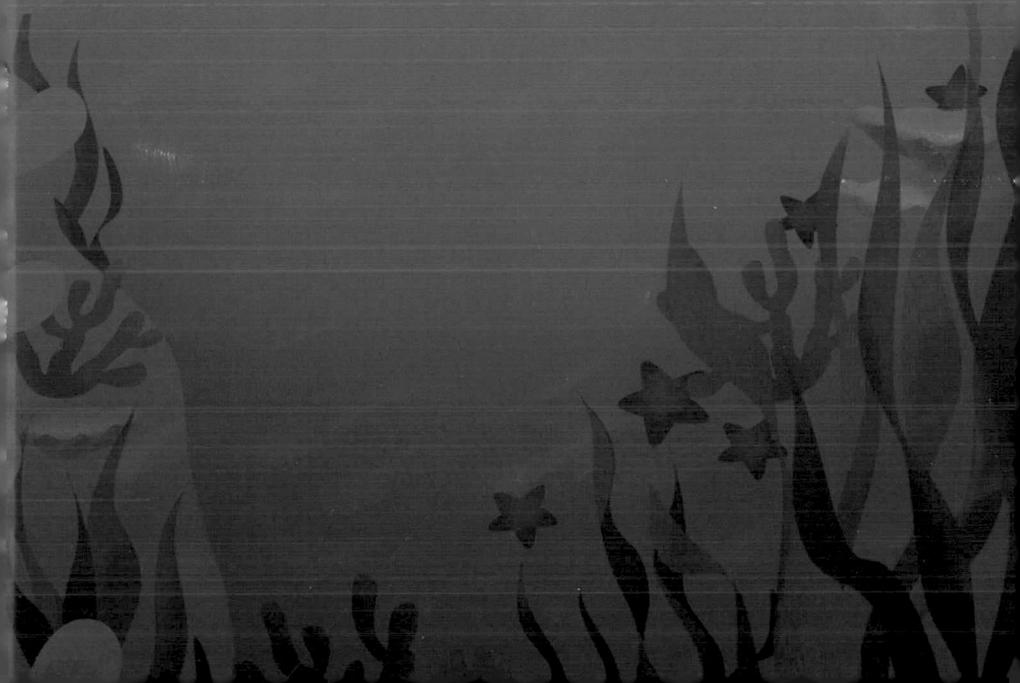

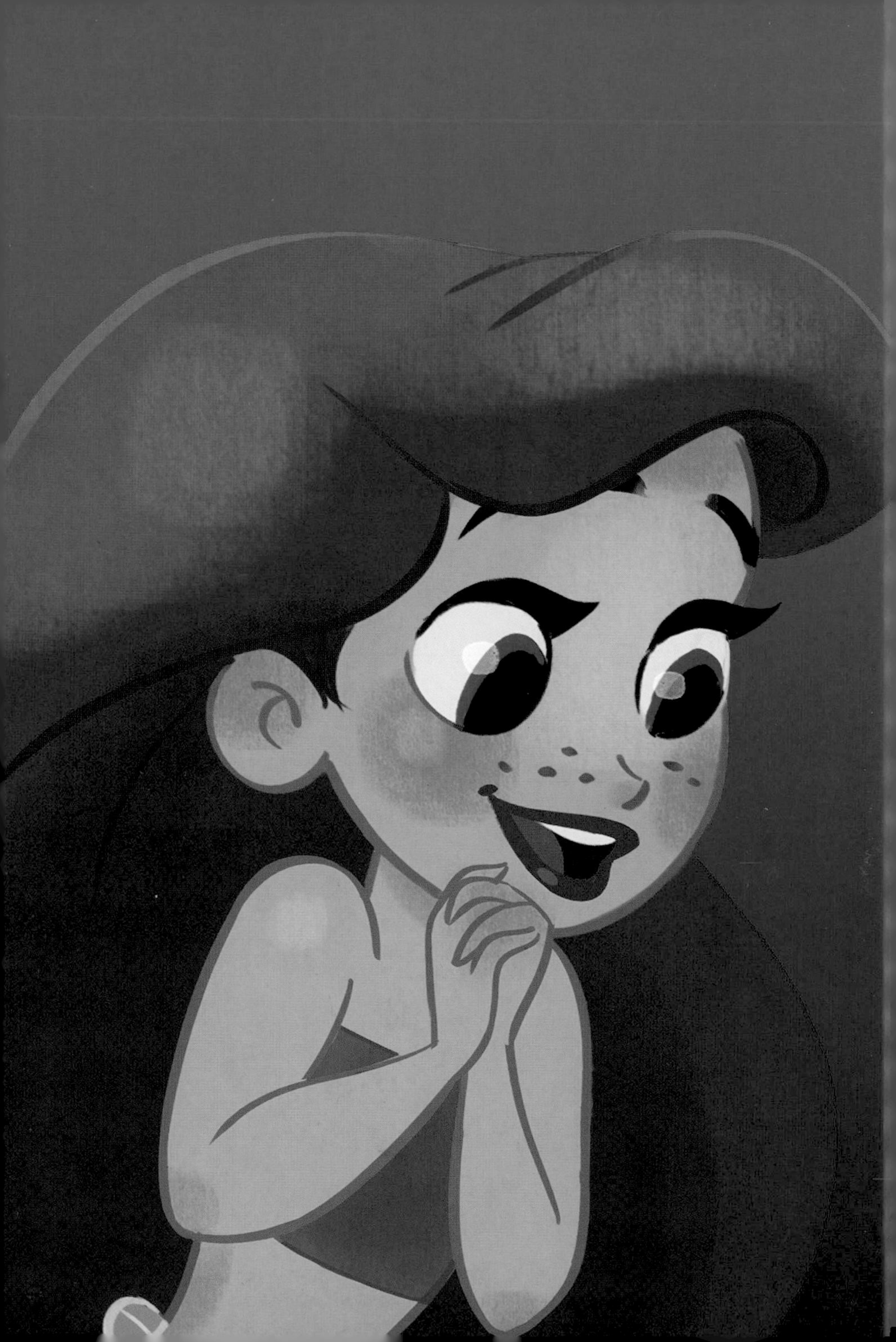

DISNEY PRINCESS

Ariel
and the
Sea Wolf

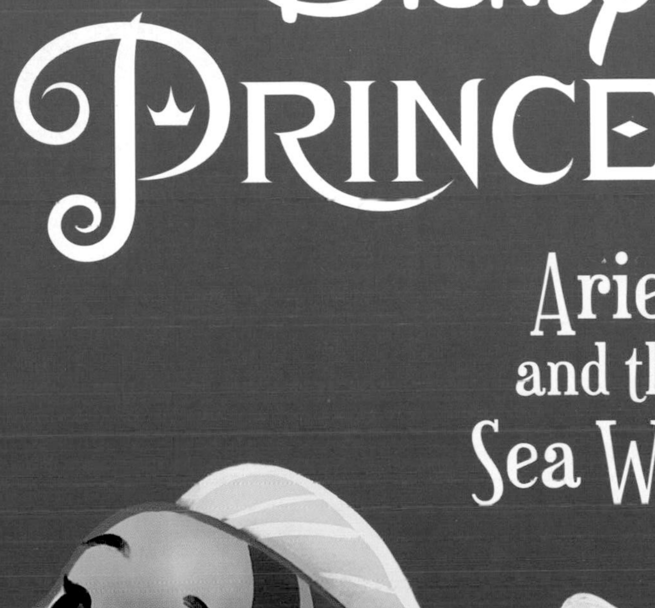

Script by
Liz Marsham

Art by
Tara Nicole Whitaker

Lettering by
Chris Dickey

Dark Horse Books

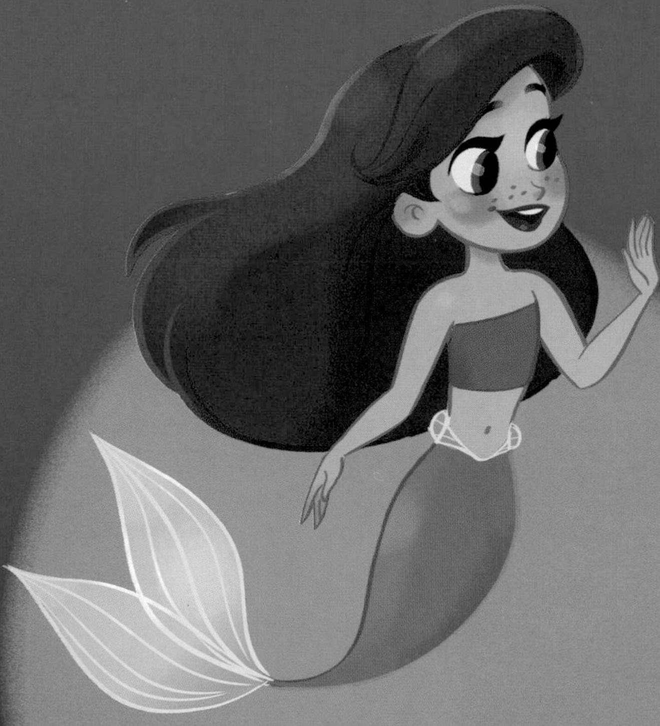

Ariel

Ariel is curious and compassionate with a wild imagination. She loves telling stories and exploring the world around her.

Aquata, Andrina, Arista, Attina, Adella, and Alana

Ariel's six older sisters are each unique in their own way. They are caring, thoughtful, and kind. They look after each other and have a strong sense of family.

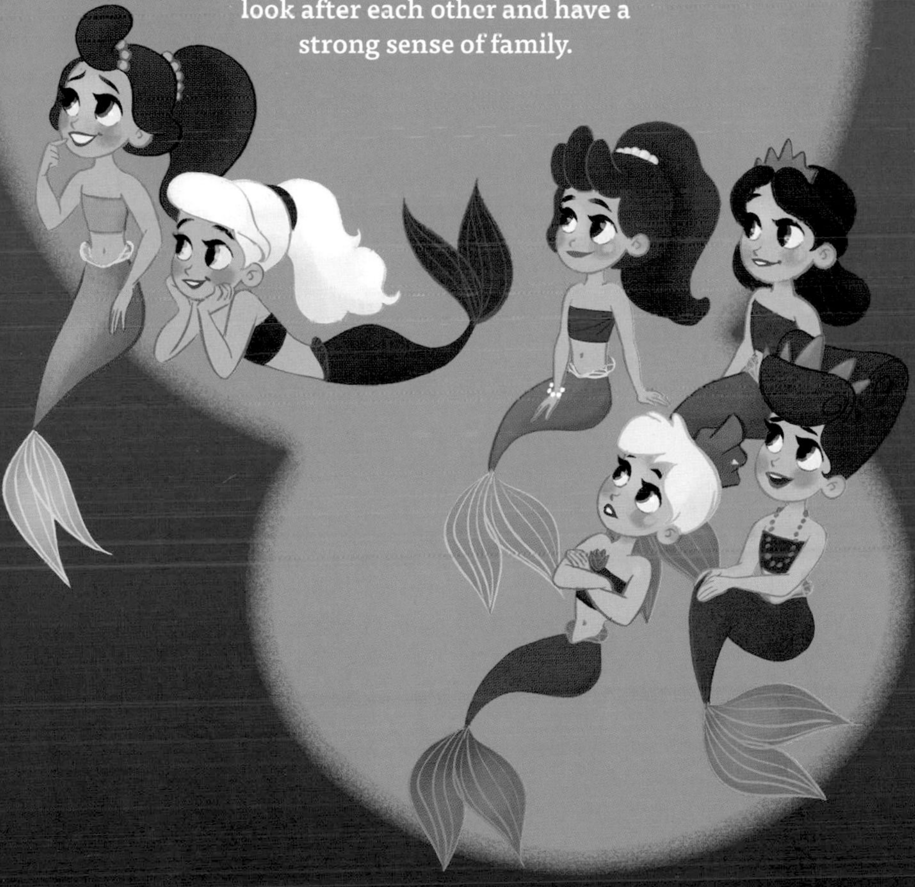

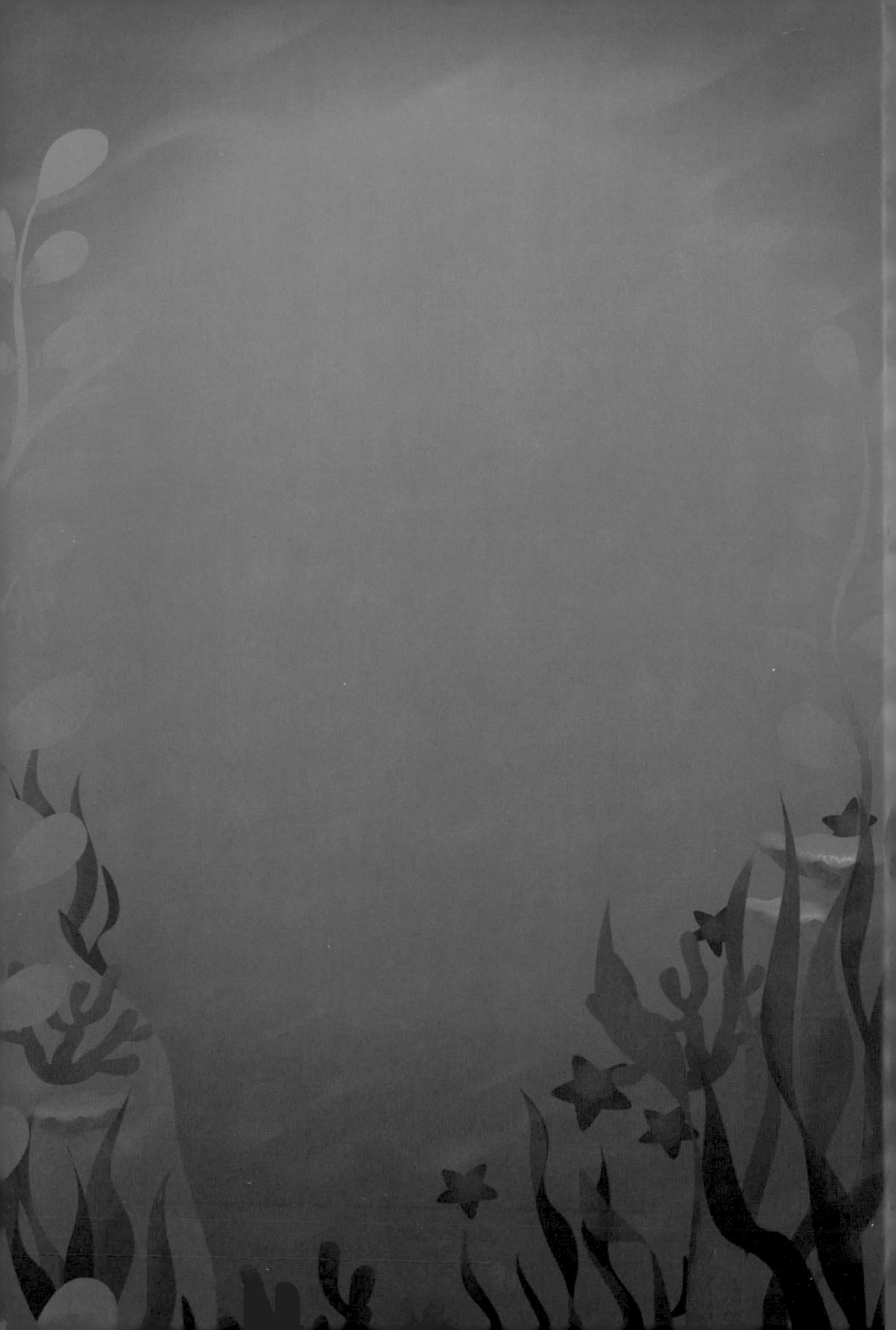

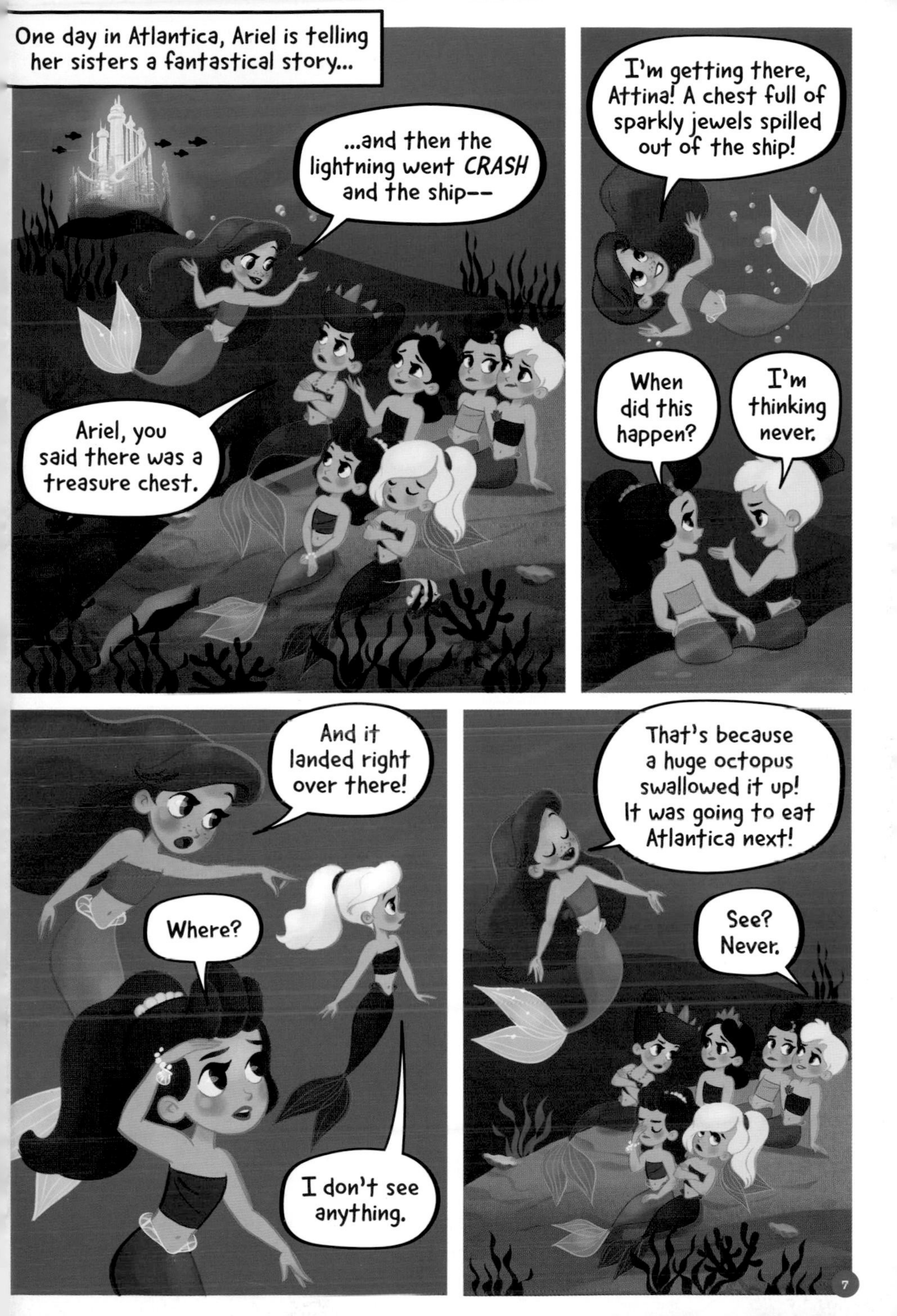

One day in Atlantica, Ariel is telling her sisters a fantastical story...
...and then the lightning went *CRASH* and the ship--
Ariel, you said there was a treasure chest.
I'm getting there, Attina! A chest full of sparkly jewels spilled out of the ship!
When did this happen?
I'm thinking never.
And it landed right over there!
Where?
I don't see anything.
That's because a huge octopus swallowed it up! It was going to eat Atlantica next!
See? Never.

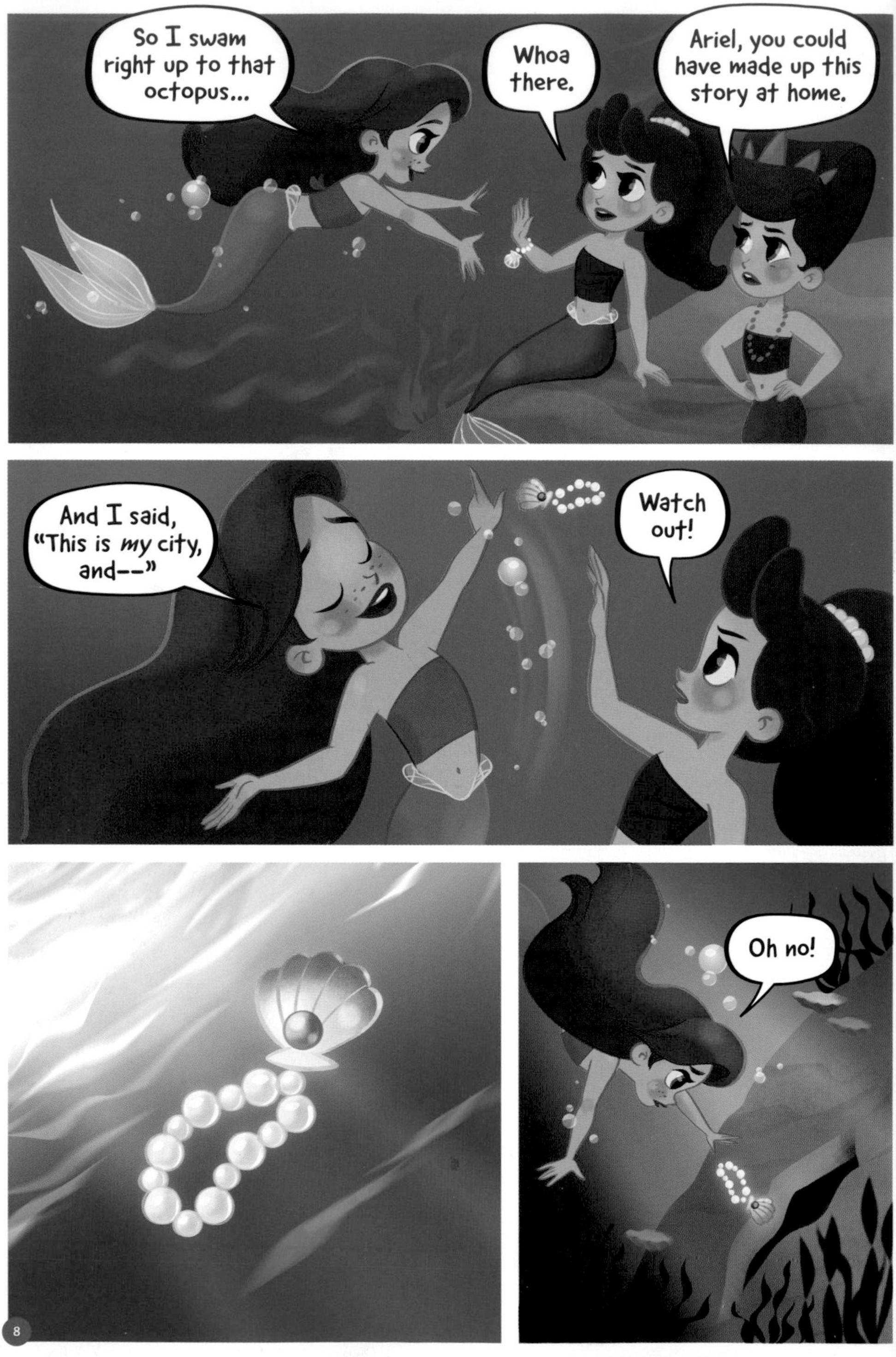
So I swam right up to that octopus...
Whoa there.
Ariel, you could have made up this story at home.
And I said, "This is *my* city, and--"
Watch out!
Oh no!

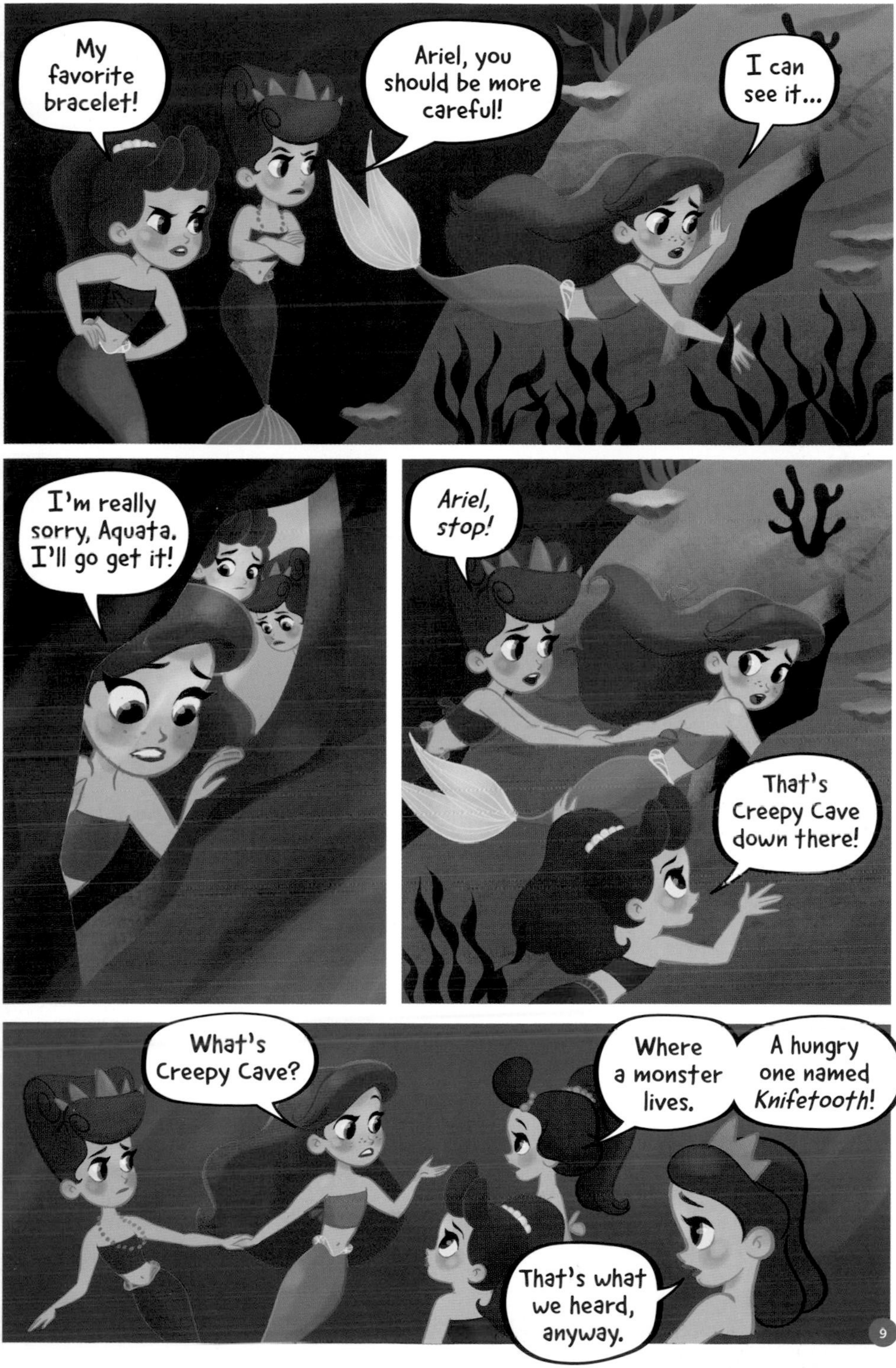
My favorite bracelet!
Ariel, you should be more careful!
I can see it...
I'm really sorry, Aquata. I'll go get it!
Ariel, stop!
That's Creepy Cave down there!
What's Creepy Cave?
Where a monster lives.
A hungry one named *Knifetooth*!
That's what we heard, anyway.

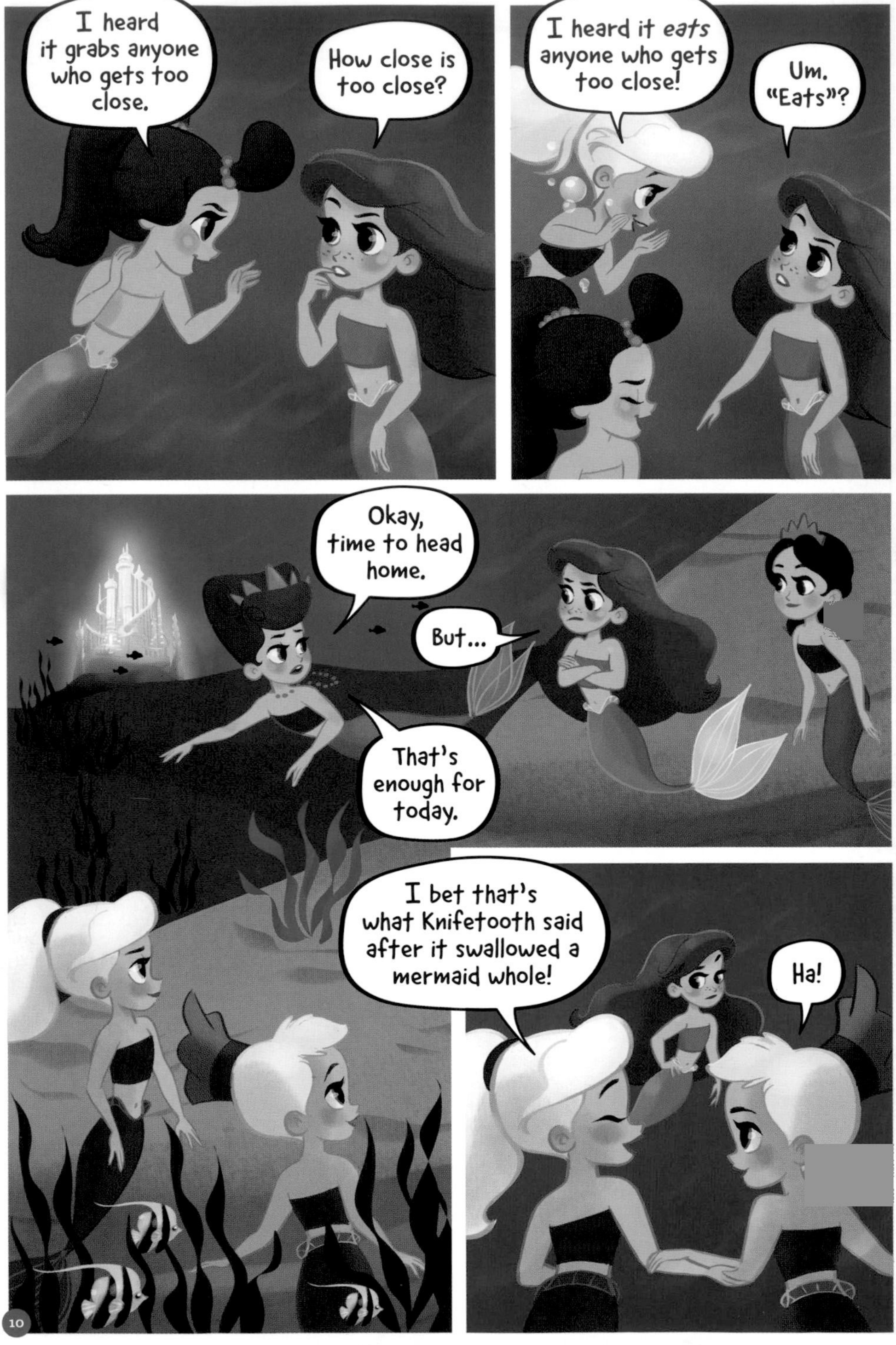
I heard it grabs anyone who gets too close.
How close is too close?
I heard it *eats* anyone who gets too close!
Um. "Eats"?
Okay, time to head home.
But...
That's enough for today.
I bet that's what Knifetooth said after it swallowed a mermaid whole!
Ha!

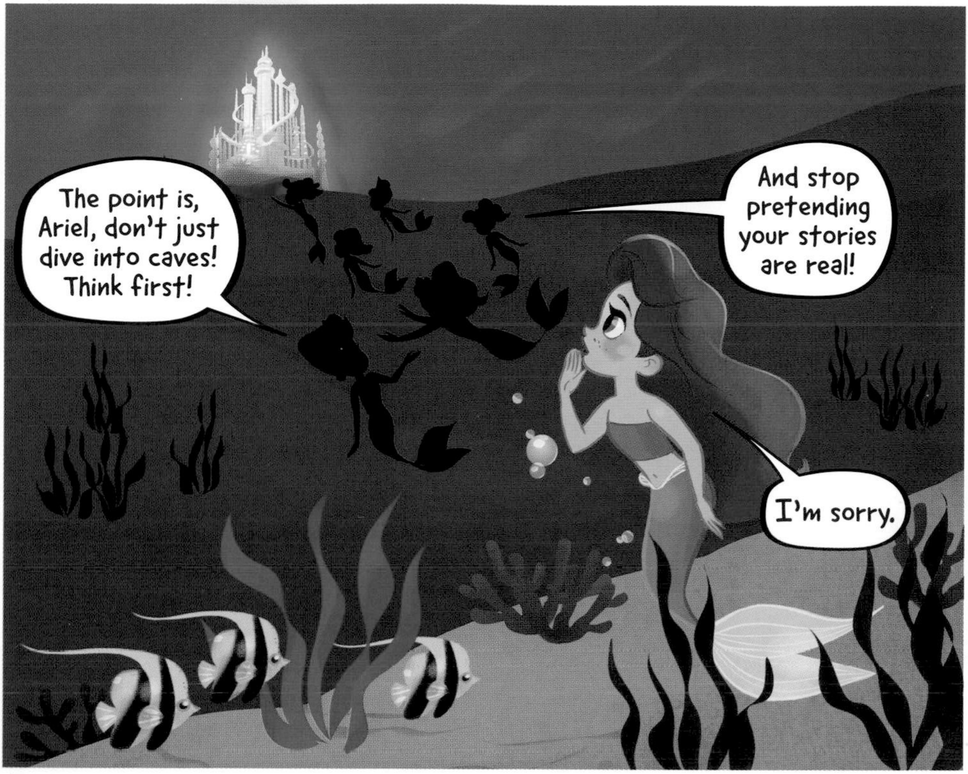
The point is, Ariel, don't just dive into caves! Think first!
And stop pretending your stories are real!
I'm sorry.

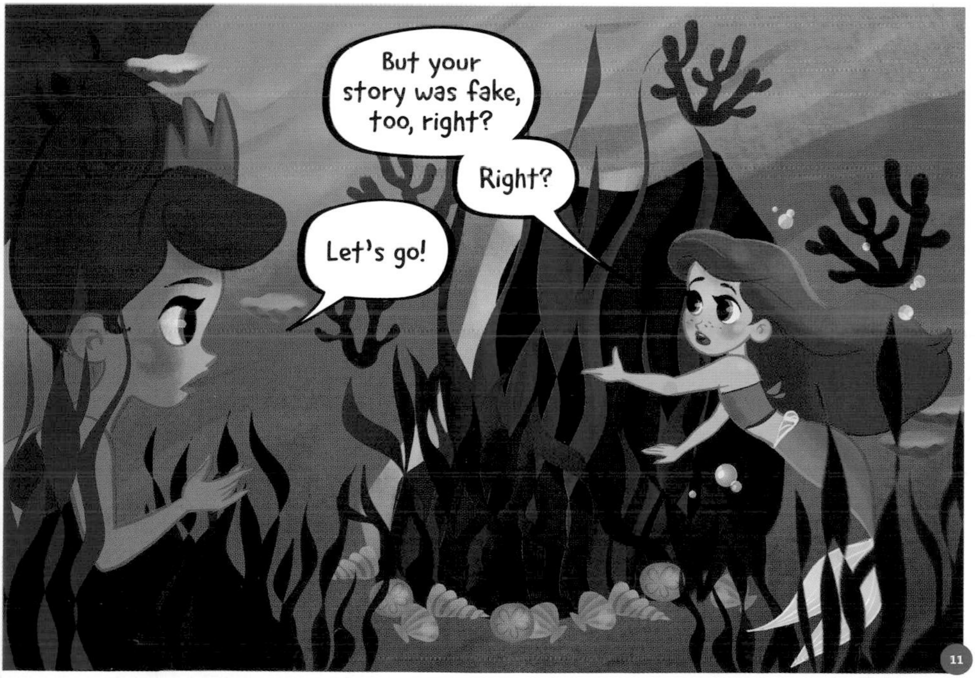
But your story was fake, too, right?
Right?
Let's go!

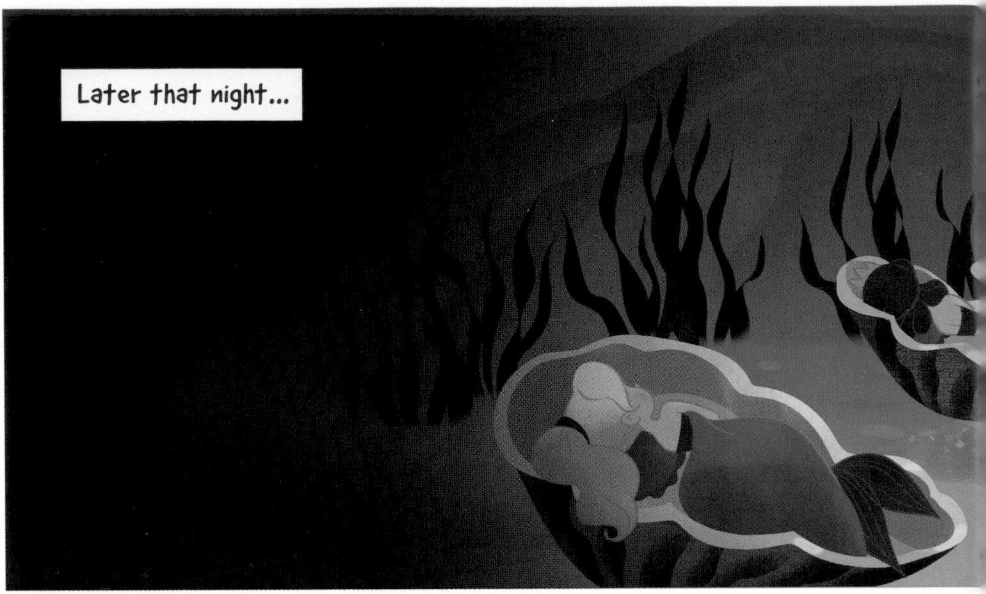
Later that night...

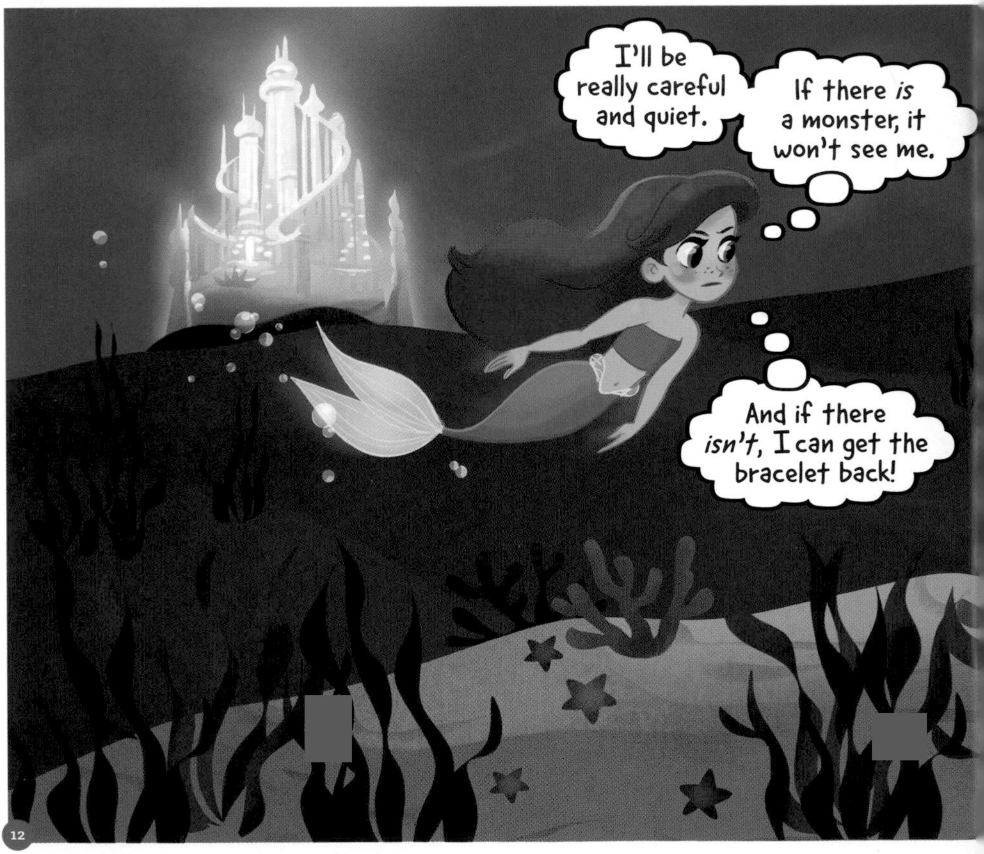
I'll be really careful and quiet.
If there *is* a monster, it won't see me.
And if there *isn't*, I can get the bracelet back!

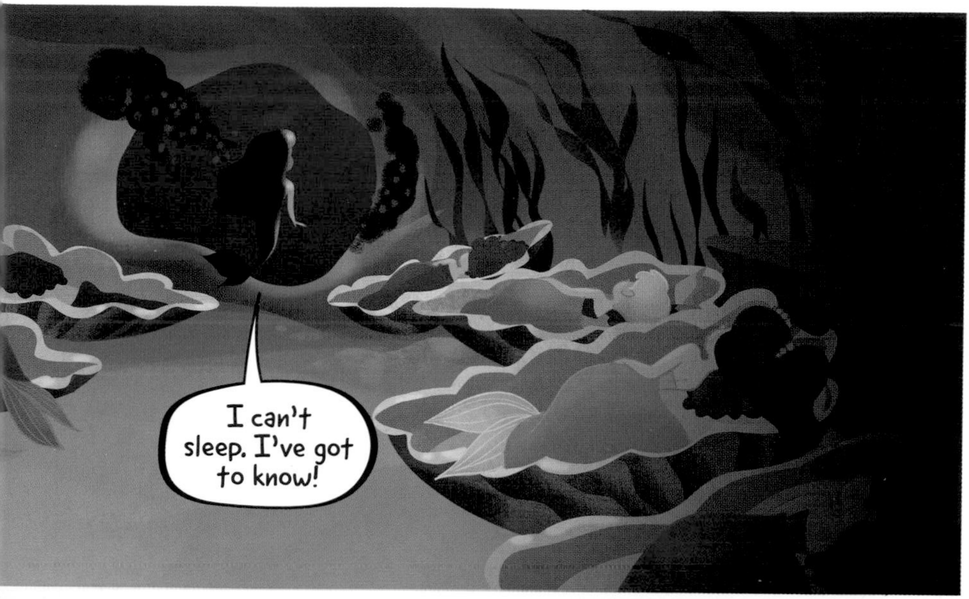
I can't sleep. I've got to know!

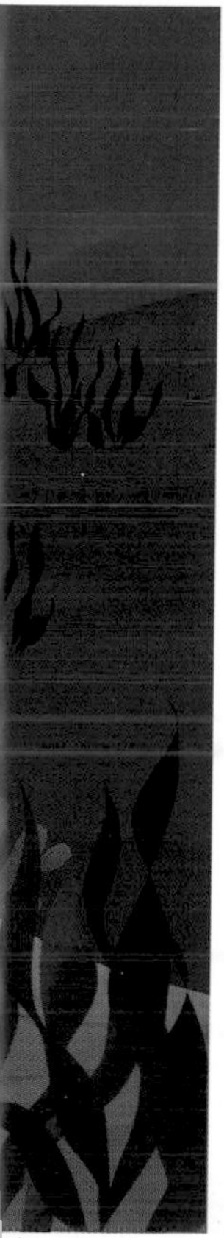

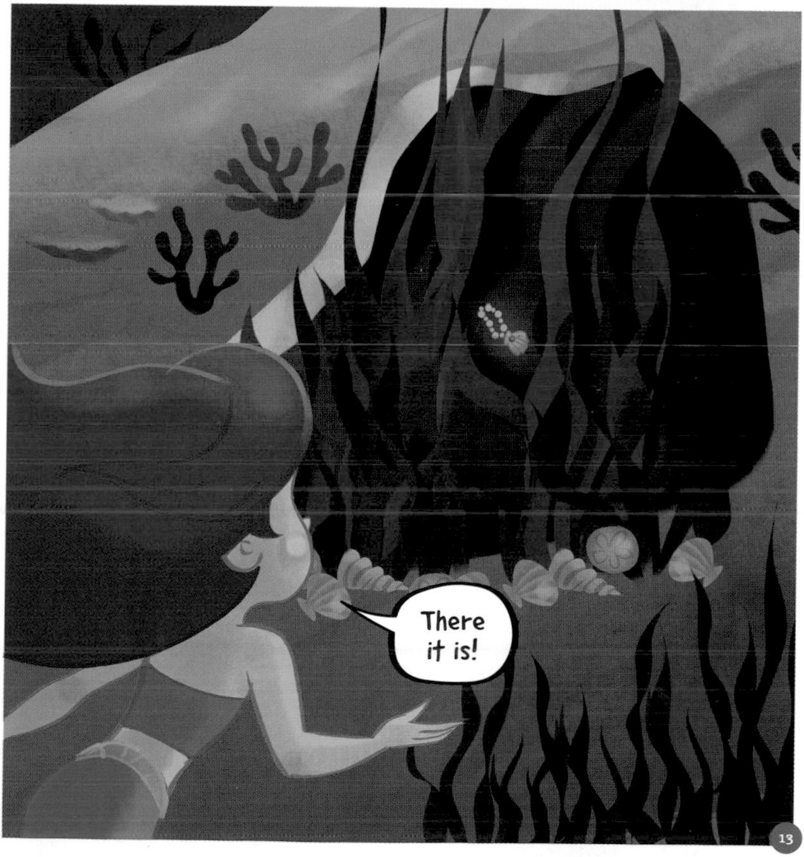
There it is!

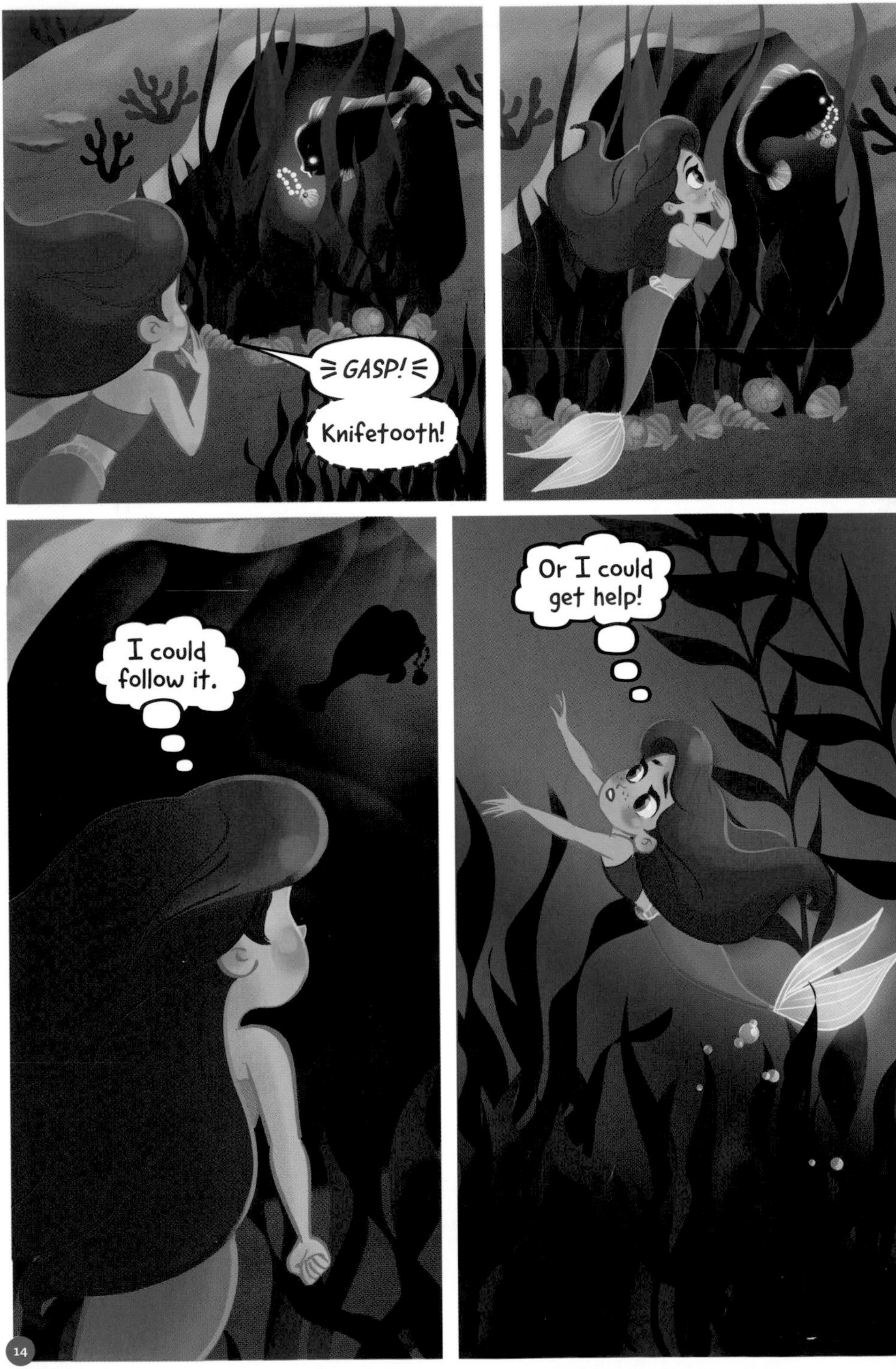
GASP!
Knifetooth!
I could follow it.
Or I could get help!

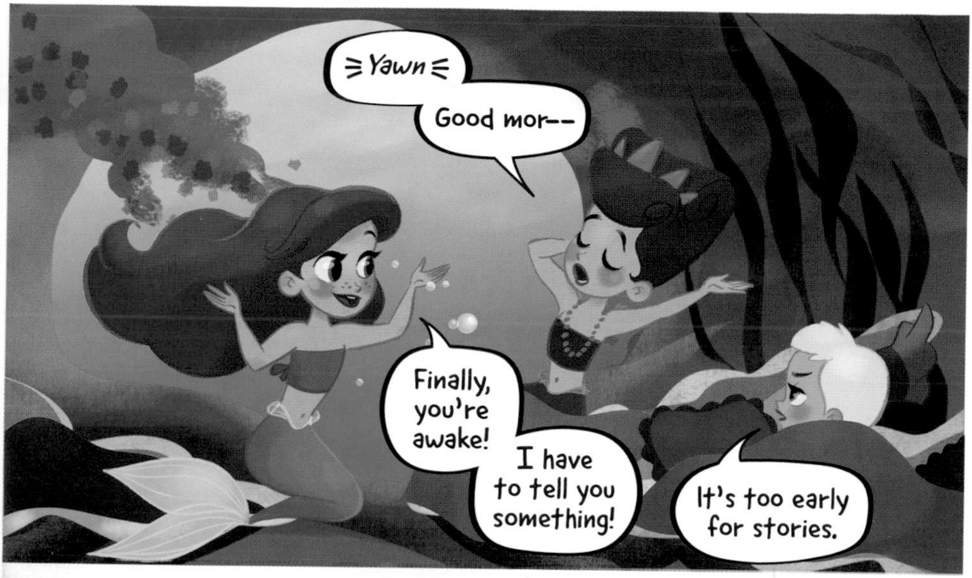
≡Yawn≡
Good mor--
Finally, you're awake!
I have to tell you something!
It's too early for stories.
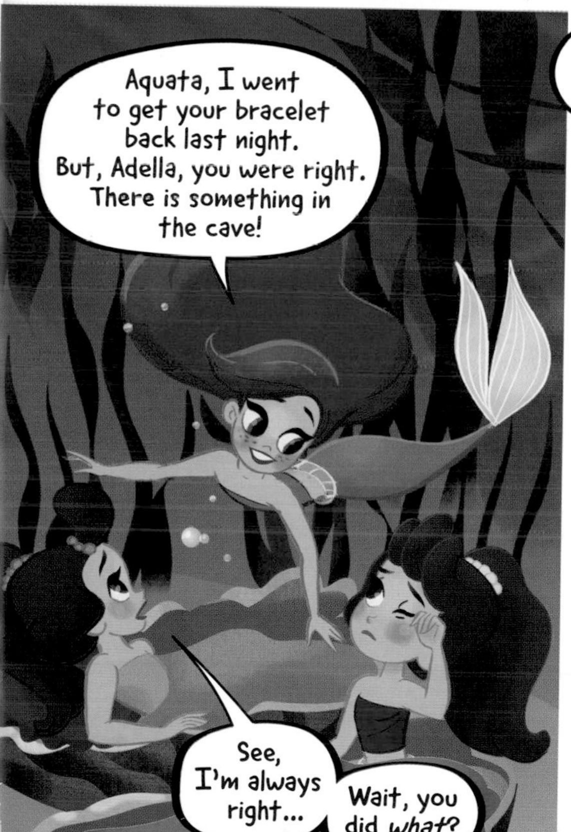
Aquata, I went to get your bracelet back last night. But, Adella, you were right. There is something in the cave!
See, I'm always right...
Wait, you did *what*?
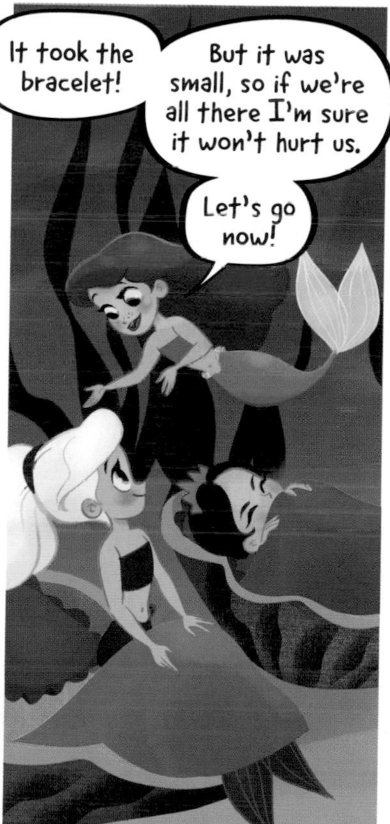
It took the bracelet!
But it was small, so if we're all there I'm sure it won't hurt us.
Let's go now!

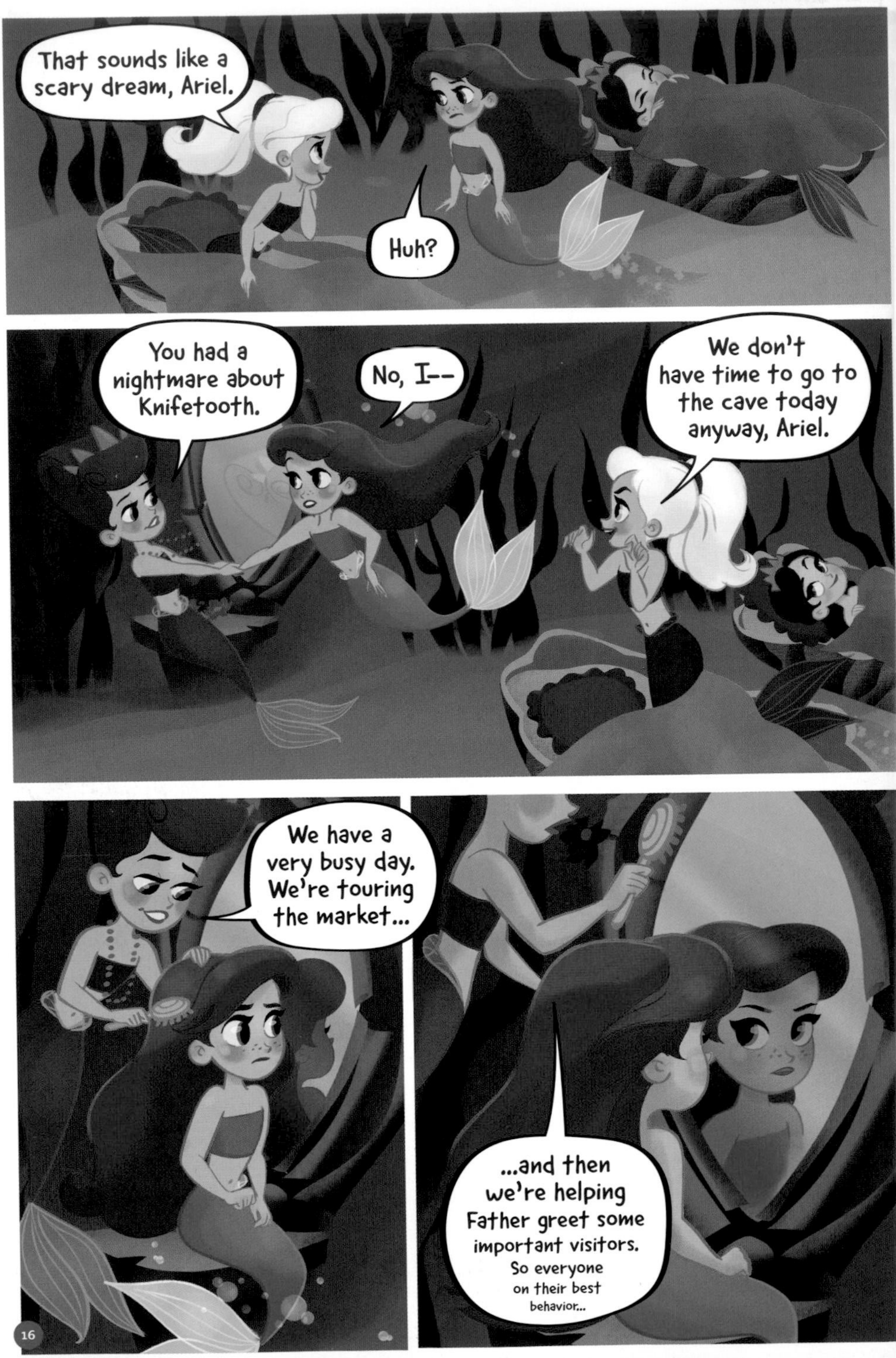
That sounds like a scary dream, Ariel.
Huh?
You had a nightmare about Knifetooth.
No, I--
We don't have time to go to the cave today anyway, Ariel.
We have a very busy day. We're touring the market...
...and then we're helping Father greet some important visitors.
So everyone on their best behavior...

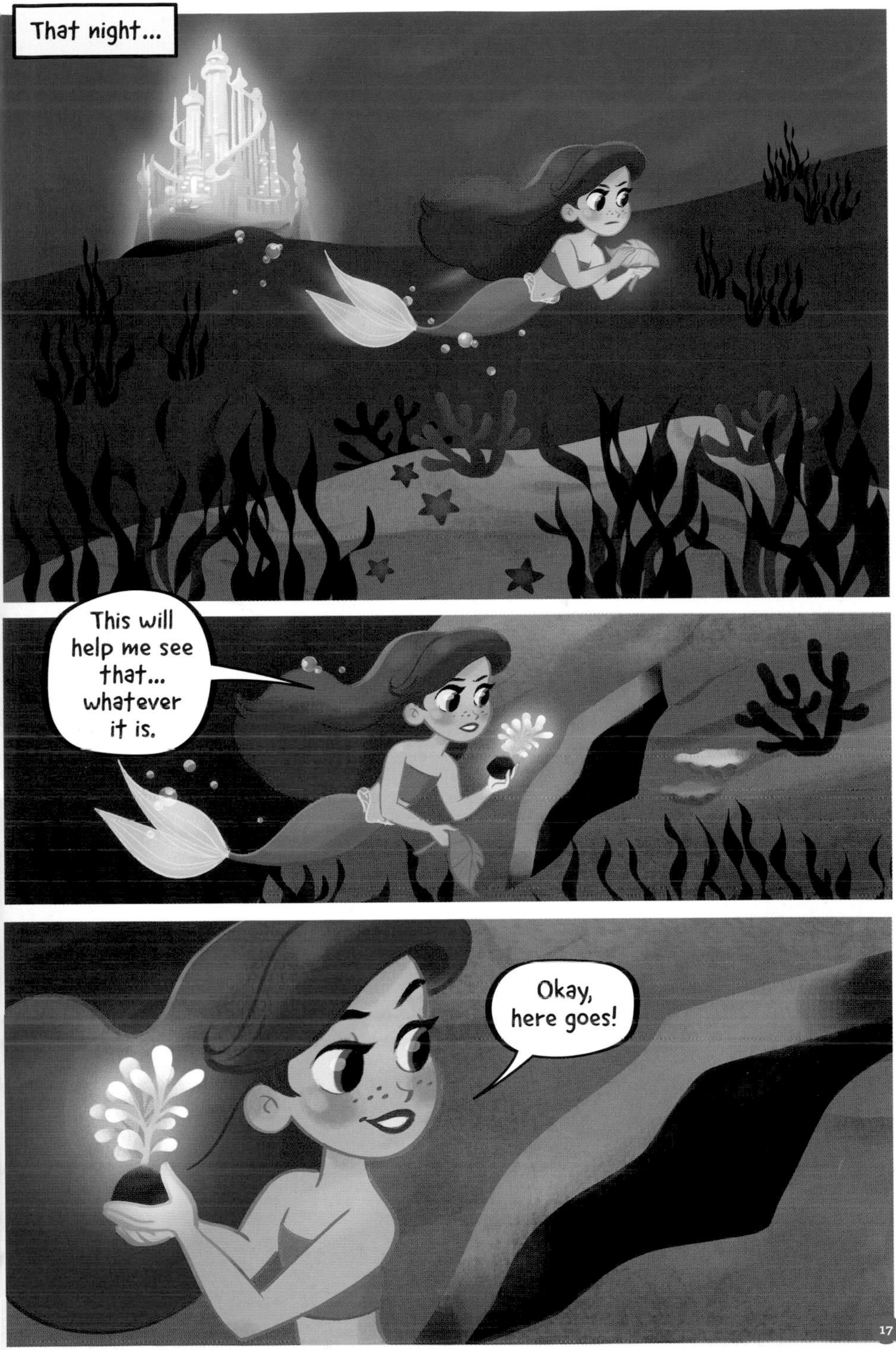
That night...
This will help me see that... whatever it is.
Okay, here goes!

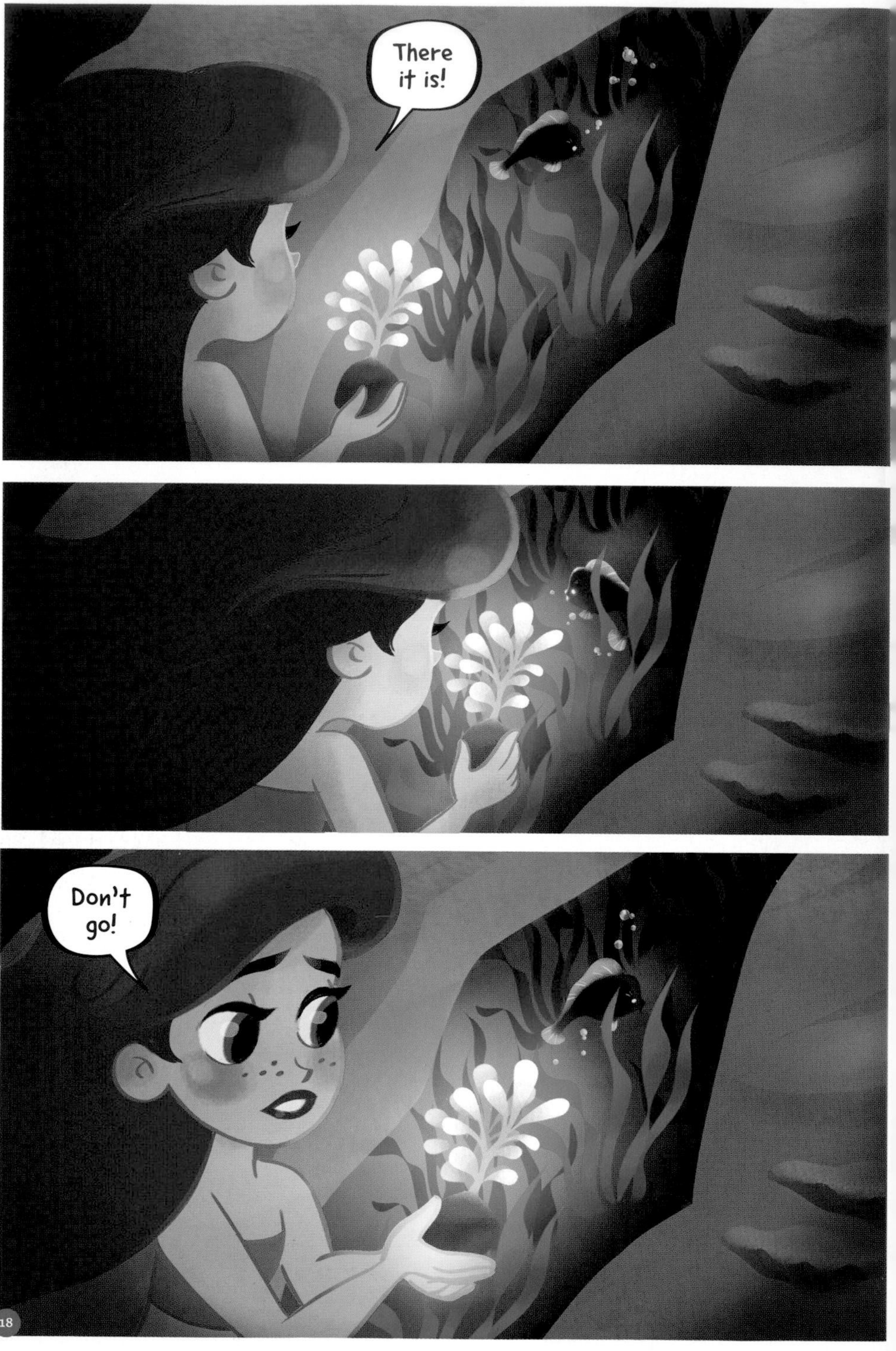
There it is!
Don't go!

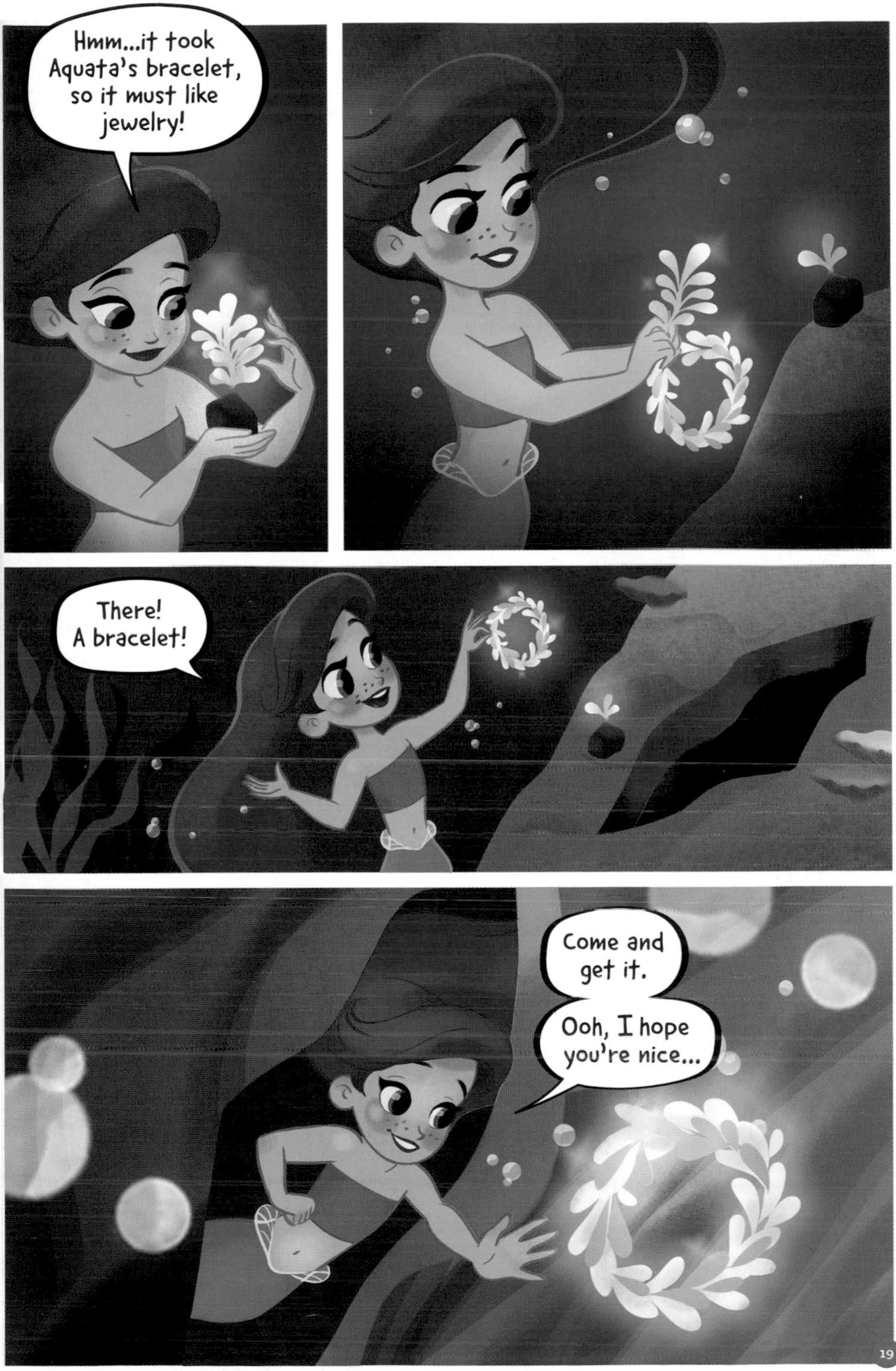

Hmm...it took Aquata's bracelet, so it must like jewelry!
There! A bracelet!
Come and get it.
Ooh, I hope you're nice...

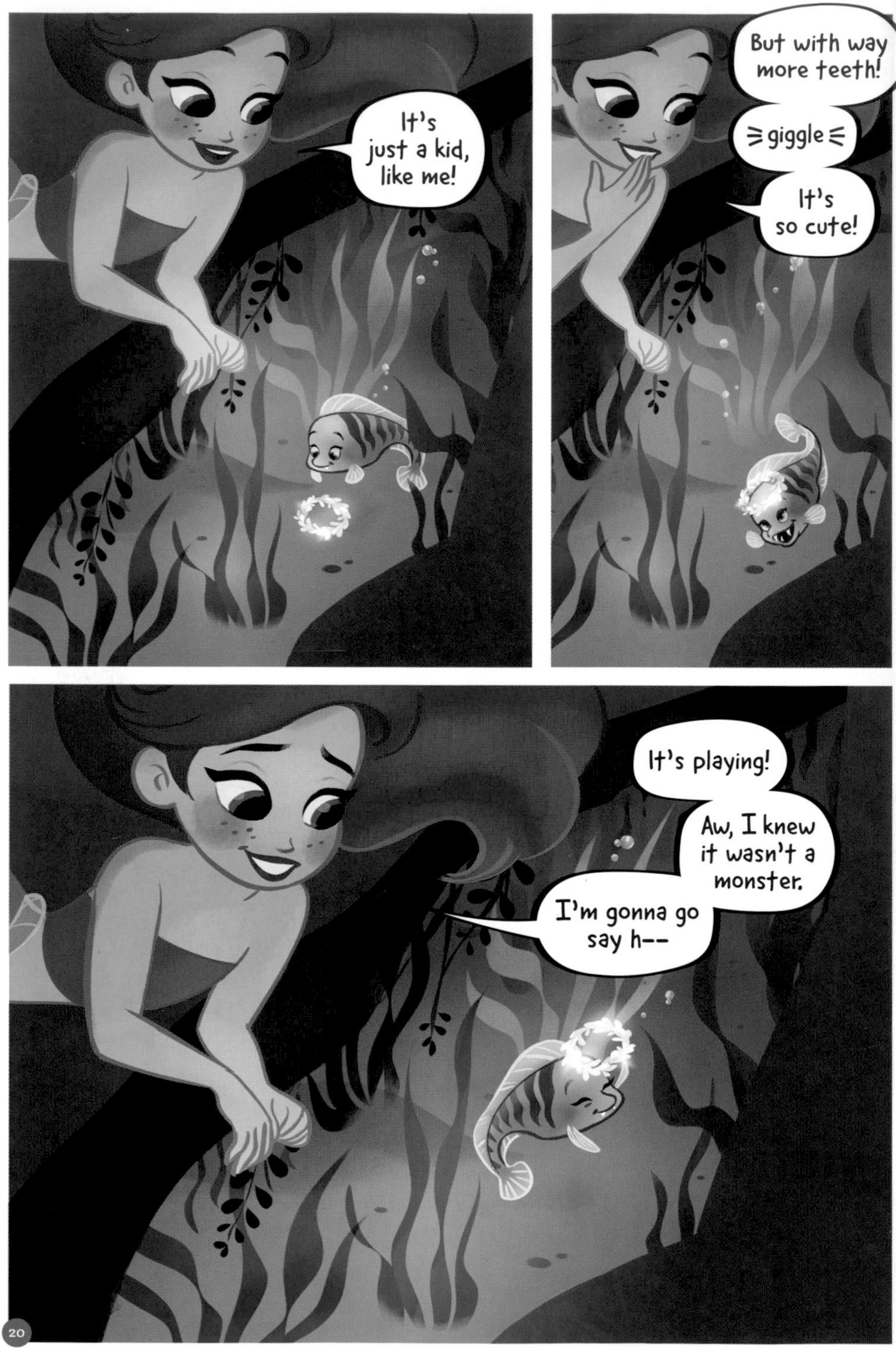
It's just a kid, like me!
But with way more teeth!
≶giggle≶
It's so cute!
It's playing!
Aw, I knew it wasn't a monster.
I'm gonna go say h--

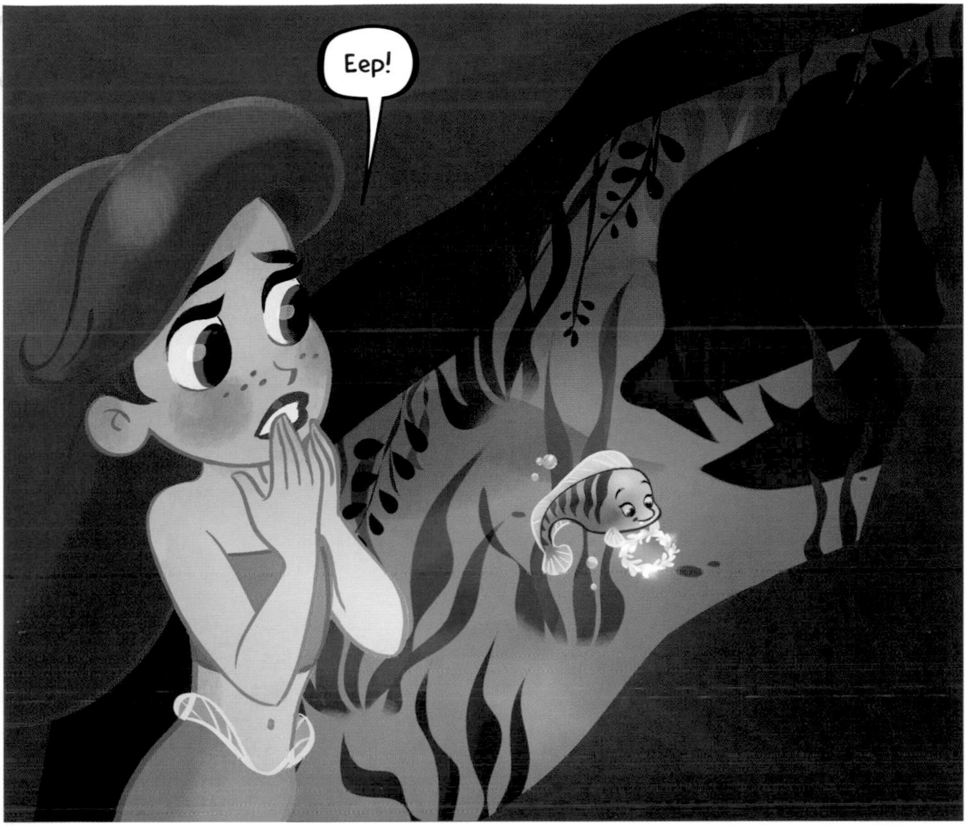
Eep!

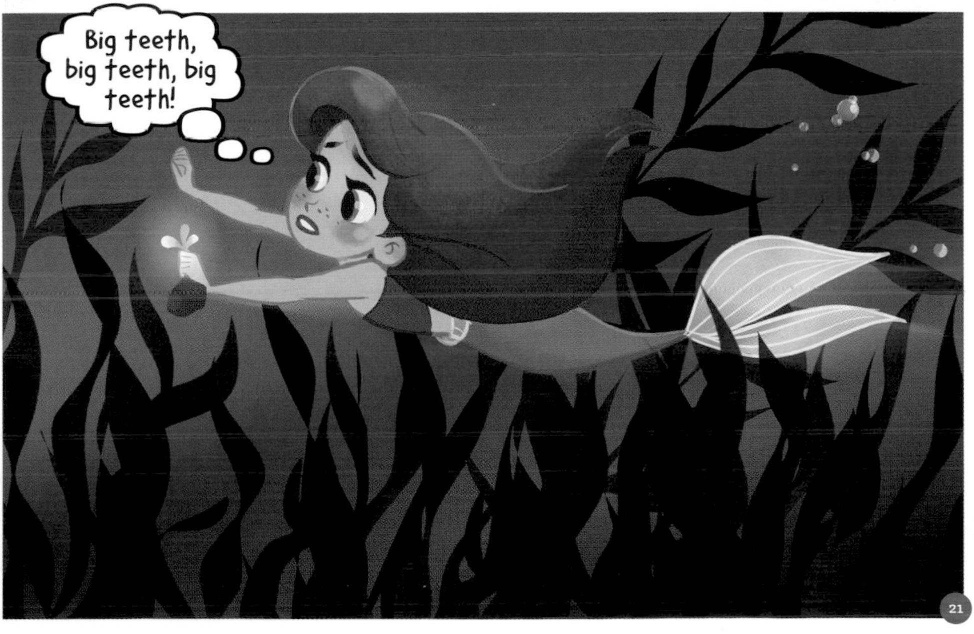
Big teeth, big teeth, big teeth!

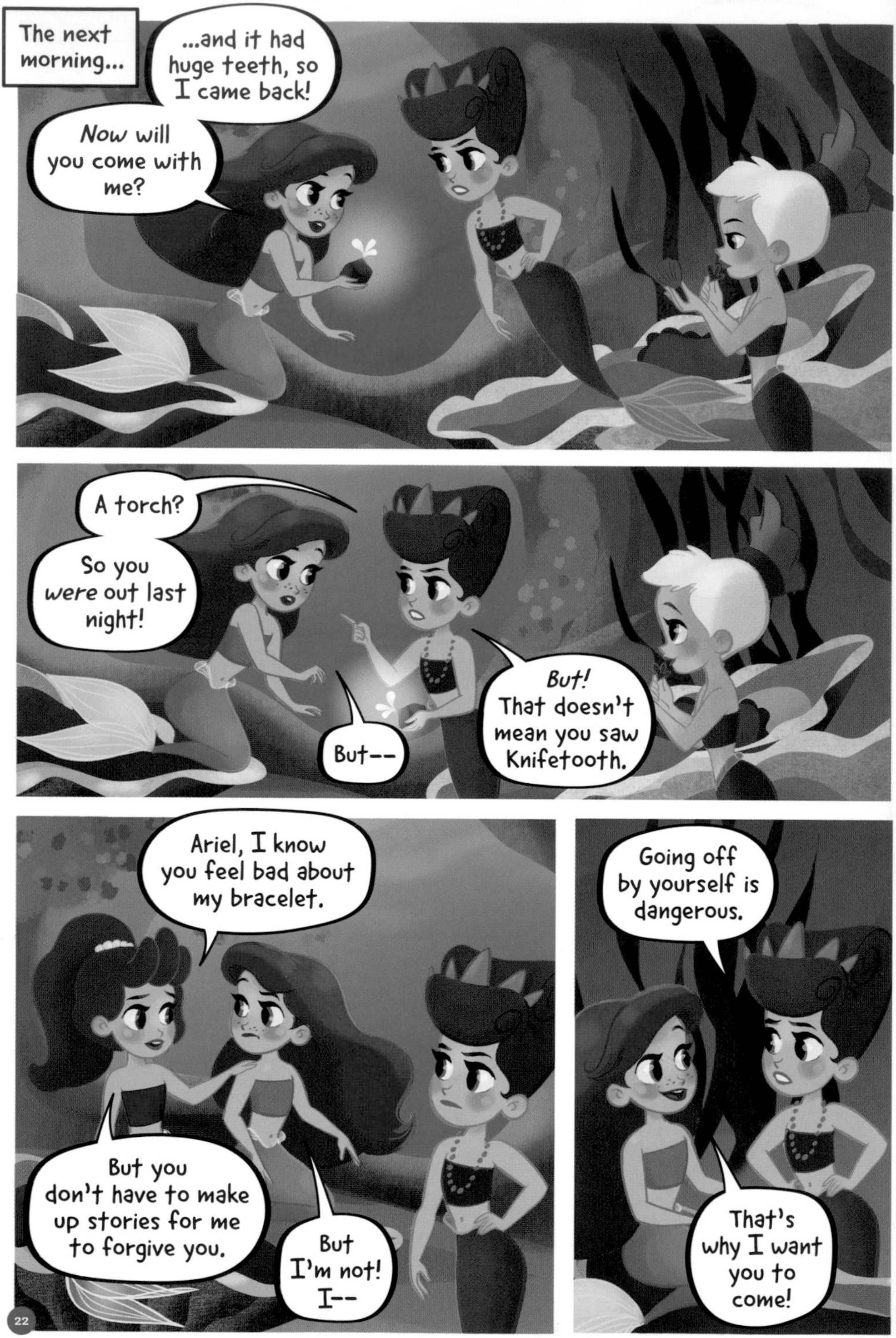
The next morning...
...and it had huge teeth, so I came back!
Now will you come with me?
A torch?
So you *were* out last night!
But--
But! That doesn't mean you saw Knifetooth.
Ariel, I know you feel bad about my bracelet.
But you don't have to make up stories for me to forgive you.
But I'm not! I--
Going off by yourself is dangerous.
That's why I want you to come!

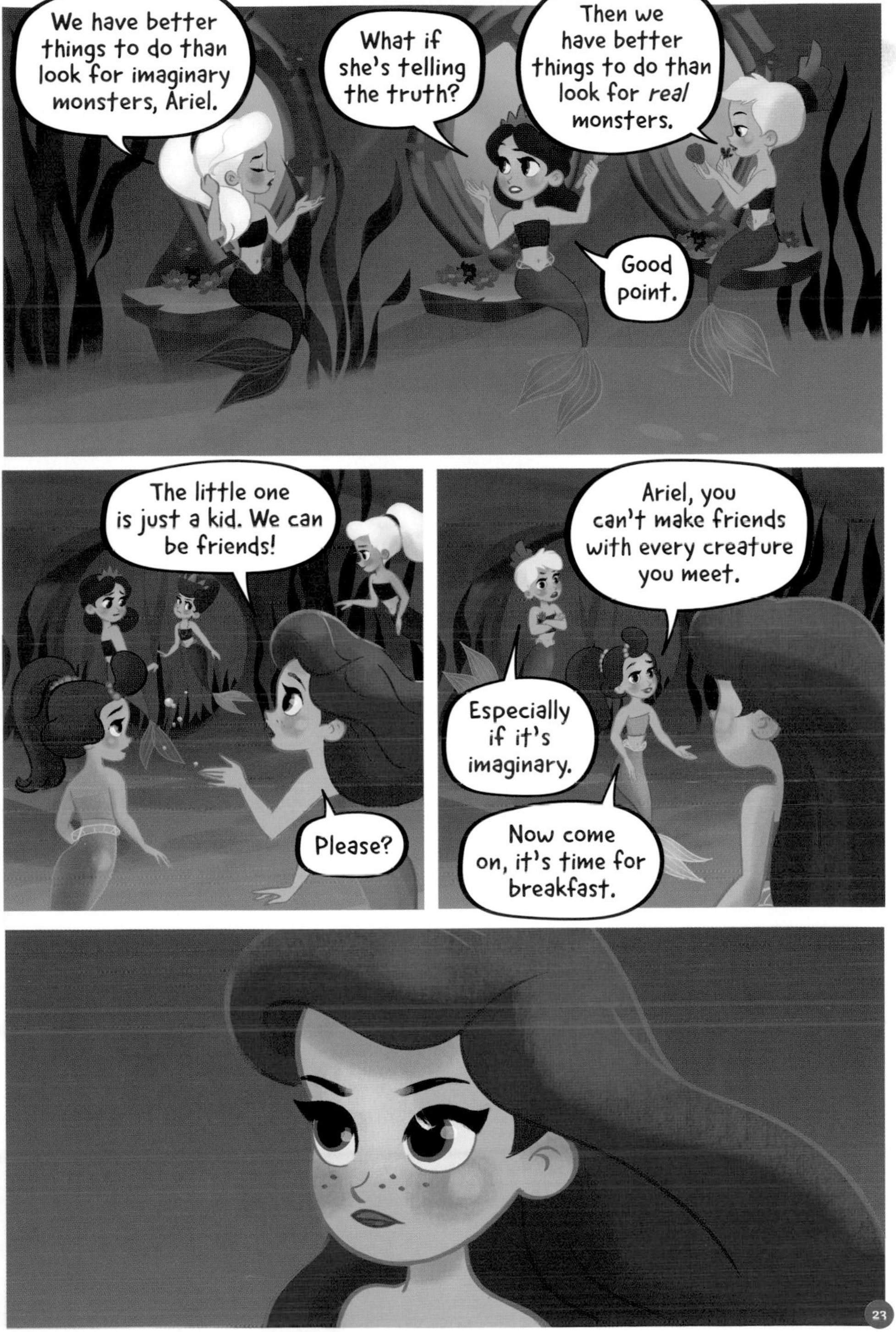

We have better things to do than look for imaginary monsters, Ariel.
What if she's telling the truth?
Then we have better things to do than look for *real* monsters.
Good point.
The little one is just a kid. We can be friends!
Please?
Ariel, you can't make friends with every creature you meet.
Especially if it's imaginary.
Now come on, it's time for breakfast.

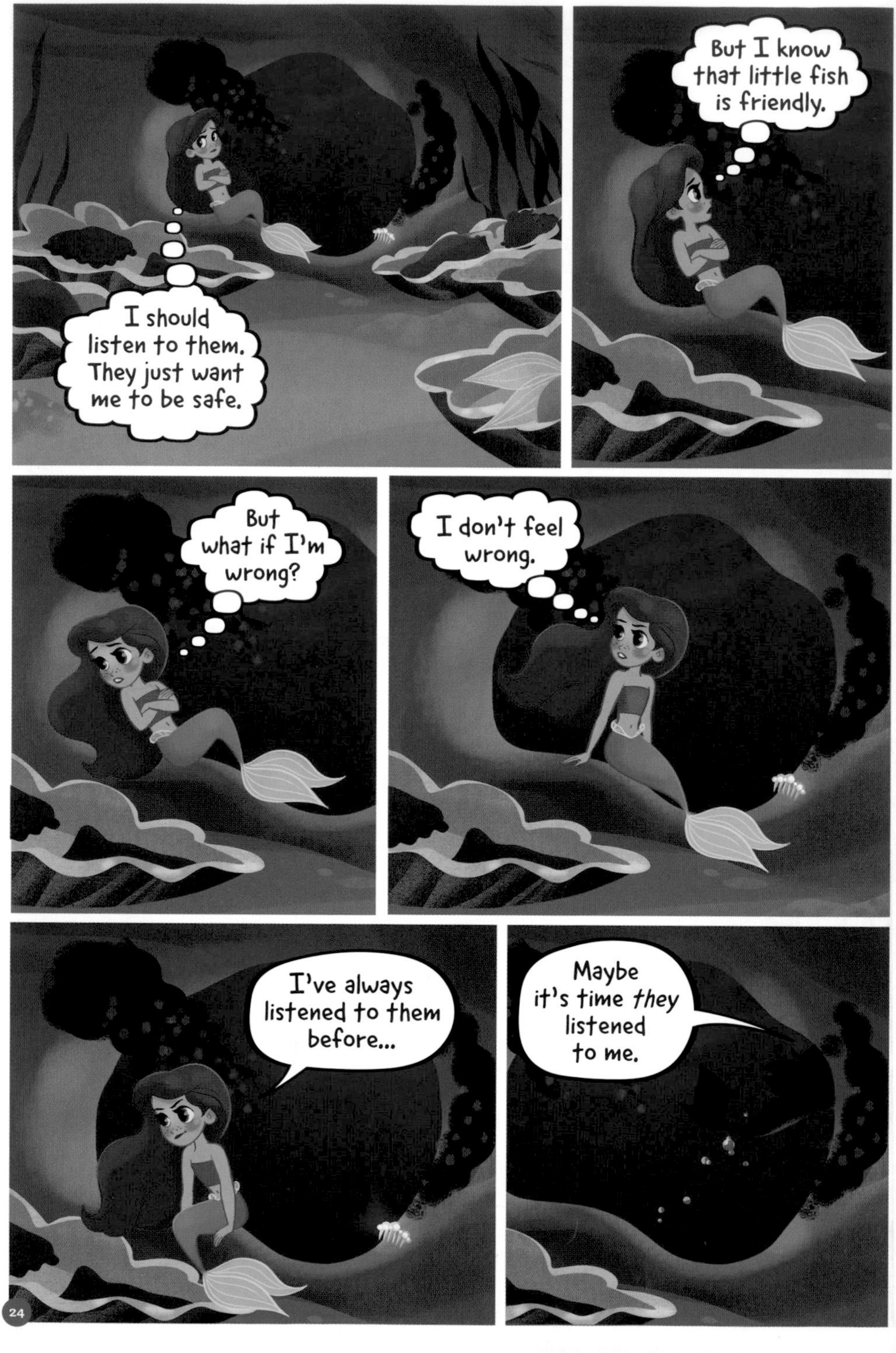
I should listen to them. They just want me to be safe.
But I know that little fish is friendly.
But what if I'm wrong?
I don't feel wrong.
I've always listened to them before...
Maybe it's time *they* listened to me.

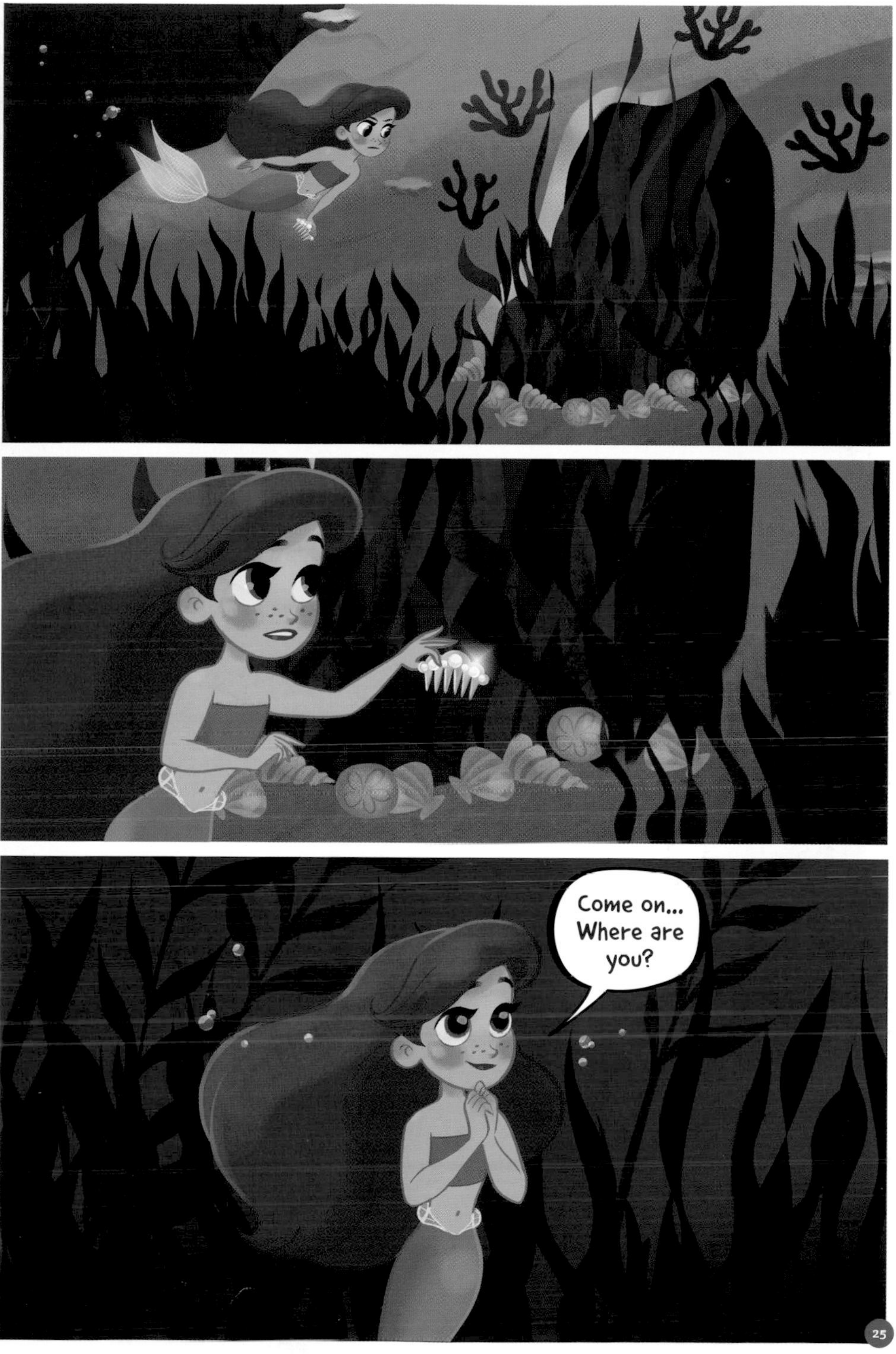
Come on... Where are you?

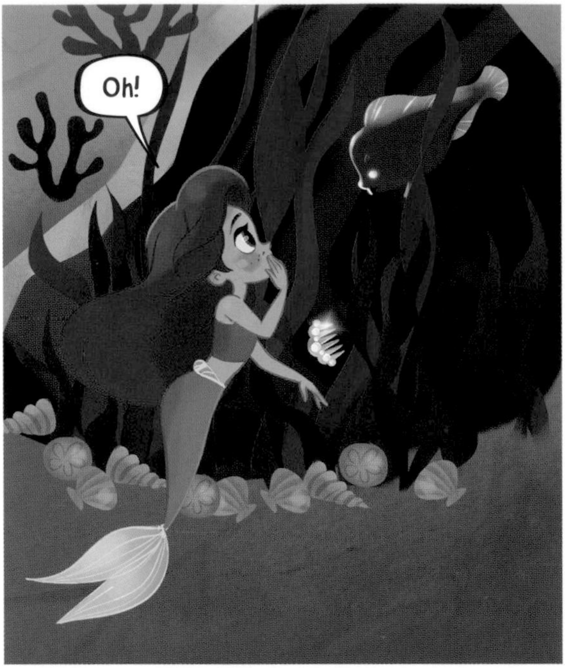
Oh!

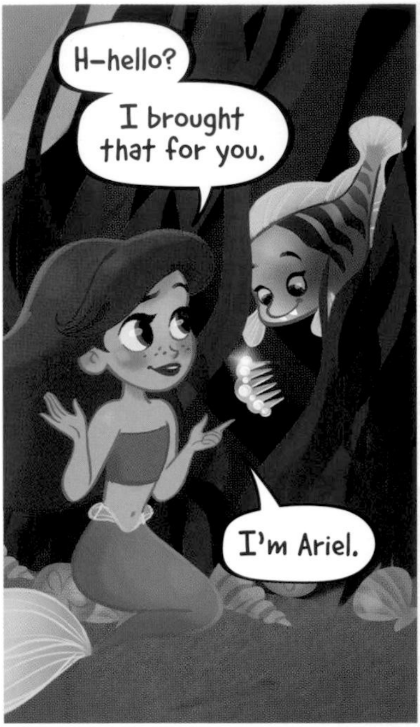
H–hello?
I brought that for you.
I'm Ariel.

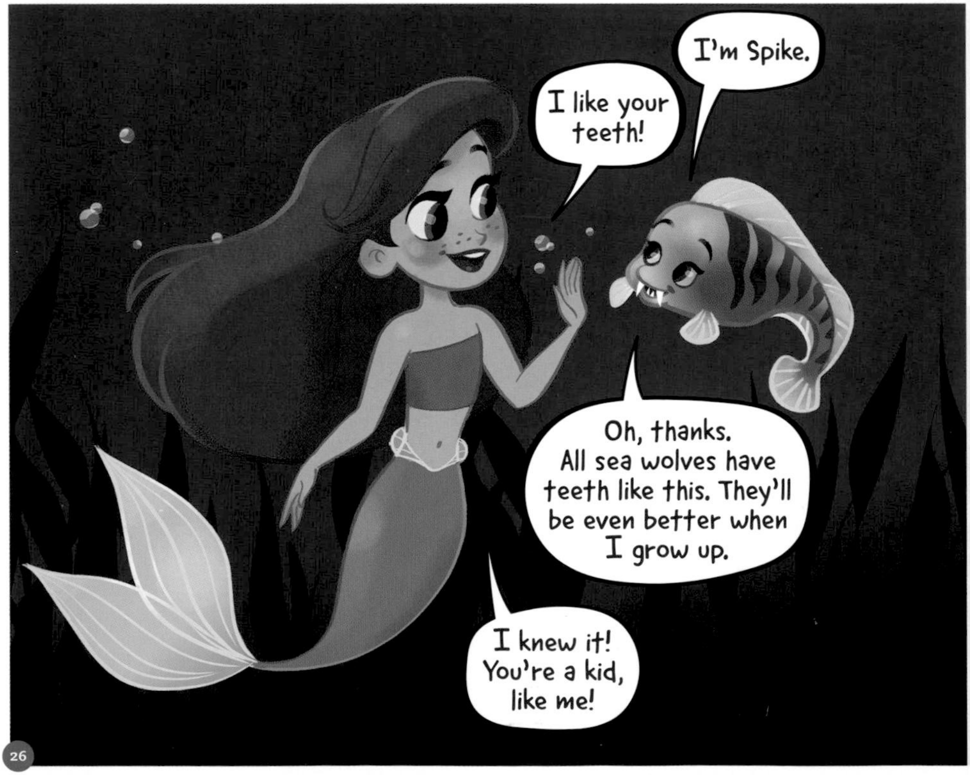
I'm Spike.
I like your teeth!
Oh, thanks. All sea wolves have teeth like this. They'll be even better when I grow up.
I knew it! You're a kid, like me!

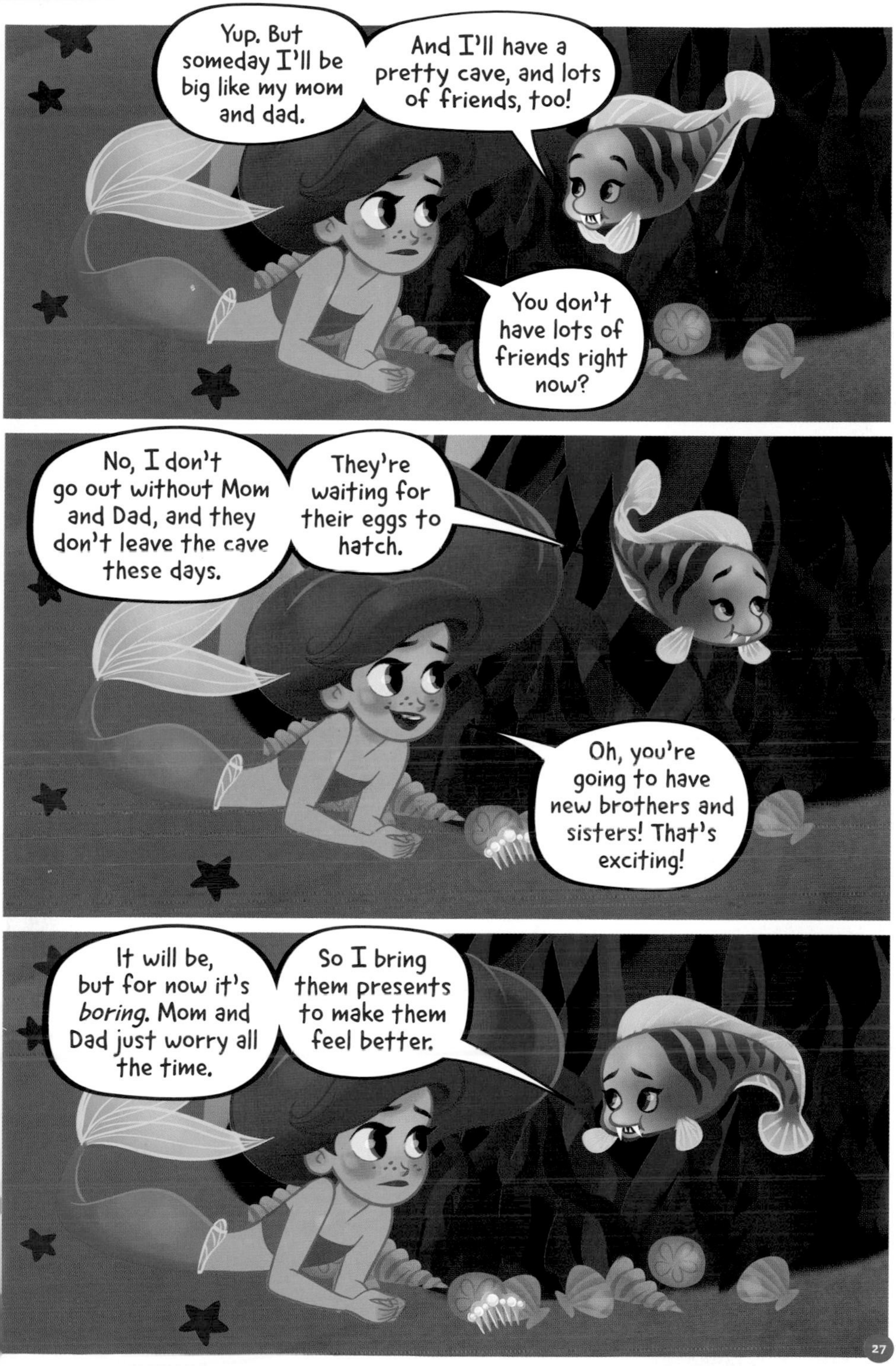
Yup. But someday I'll be big like my mom and dad.
And I'll have a pretty cave, and lots of friends, too!
You don't have lots of friends right now?
No, I don't go out without Mom and Dad, and they don't leave the cave these days.
They're waiting for their eggs to hatch.
Oh, you're going to have new brothers and sisters! That's exciting!
It will be, but for now it's *boring*. Mom and Dad just worry all the time.
So I bring them presents to make them feel better.

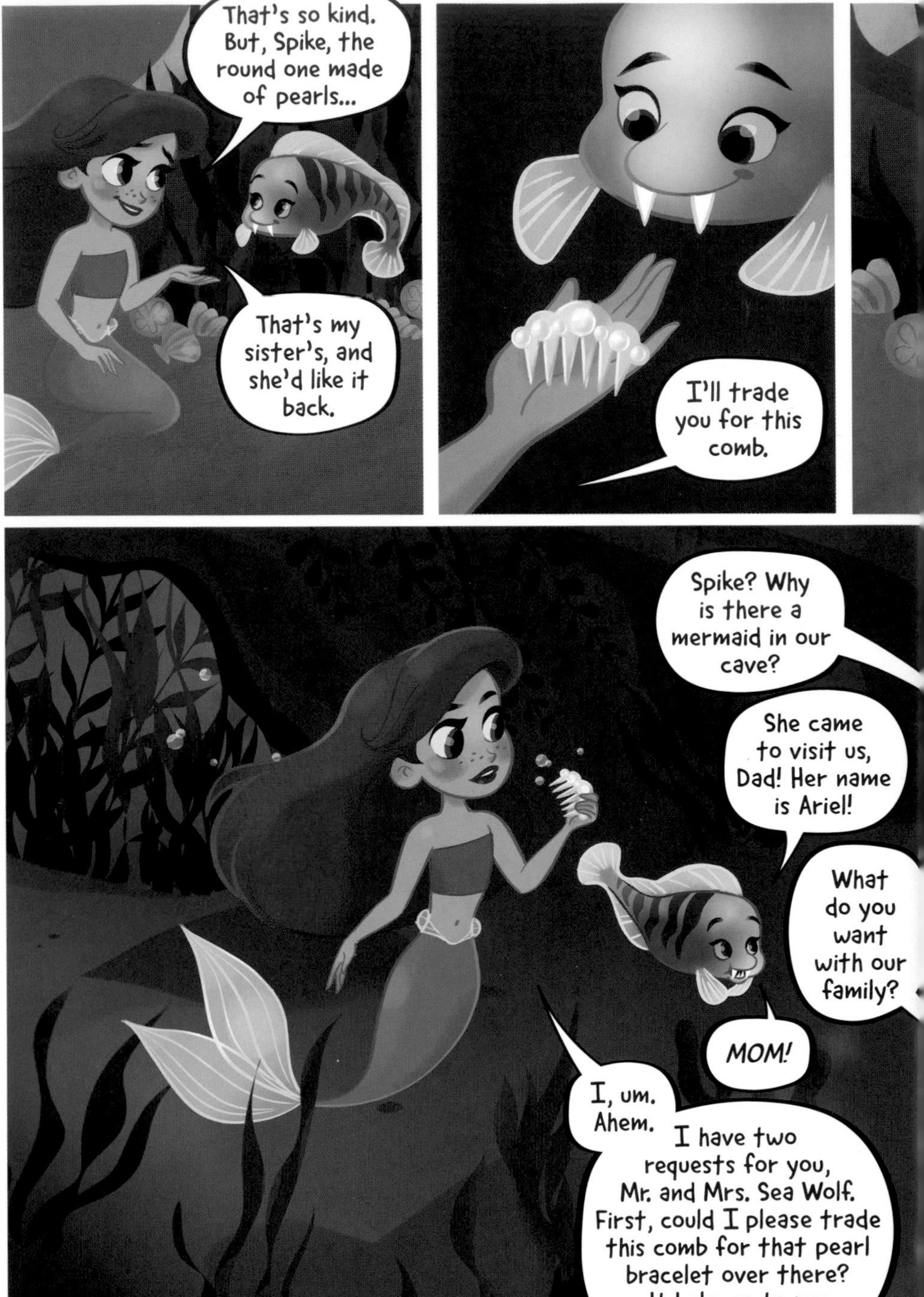
That's so kind. But, Spike, the round one made of pearls...
That's my sister's, and she'd like it back.
I'll trade you for this comb.
Spike? Why is there a mermaid in our cave?
She came to visit us, Dad! Her name is Ariel!
What do you want with our family?
MOM!
I, um. Ahem.
I have two requests for you, Mr. and Mrs. Sea Wolf. First, could I please trade this comb for that pearl bracelet over there? It belongs to my sister.

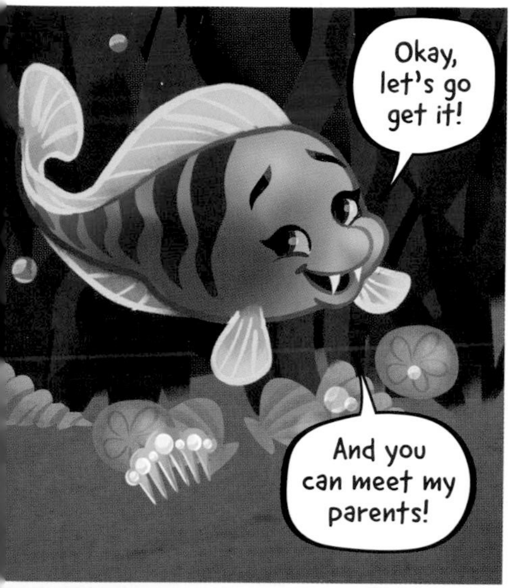
Okay, let's go get it!
And you can meet my parents!

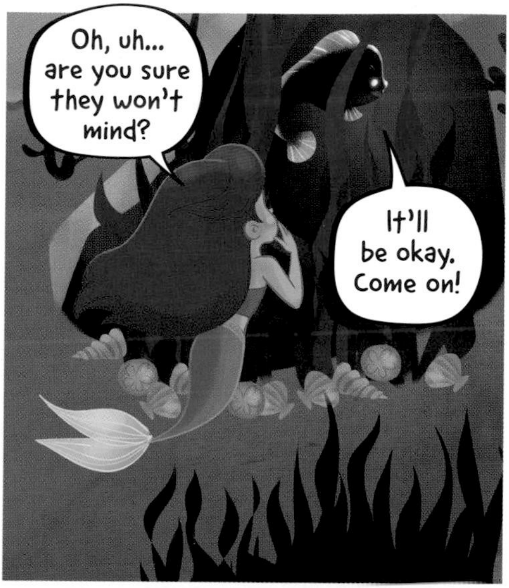
Oh, uh... are you sure they won't mind?
It'll be okay. Come on!

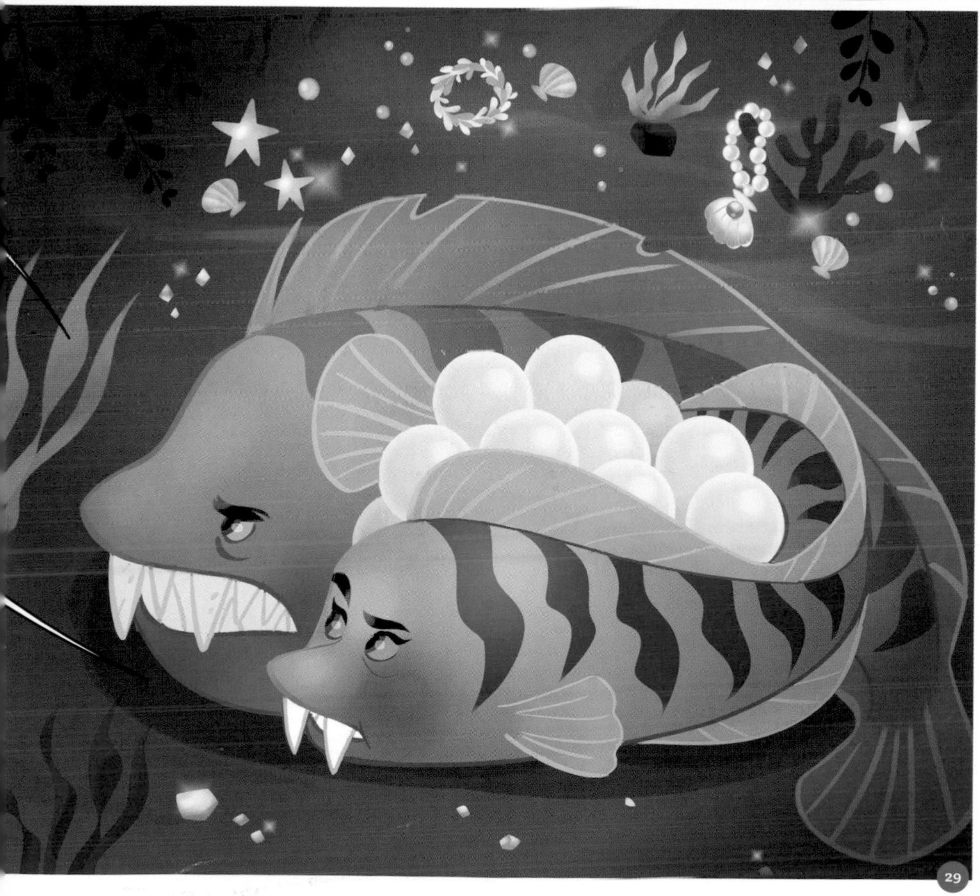

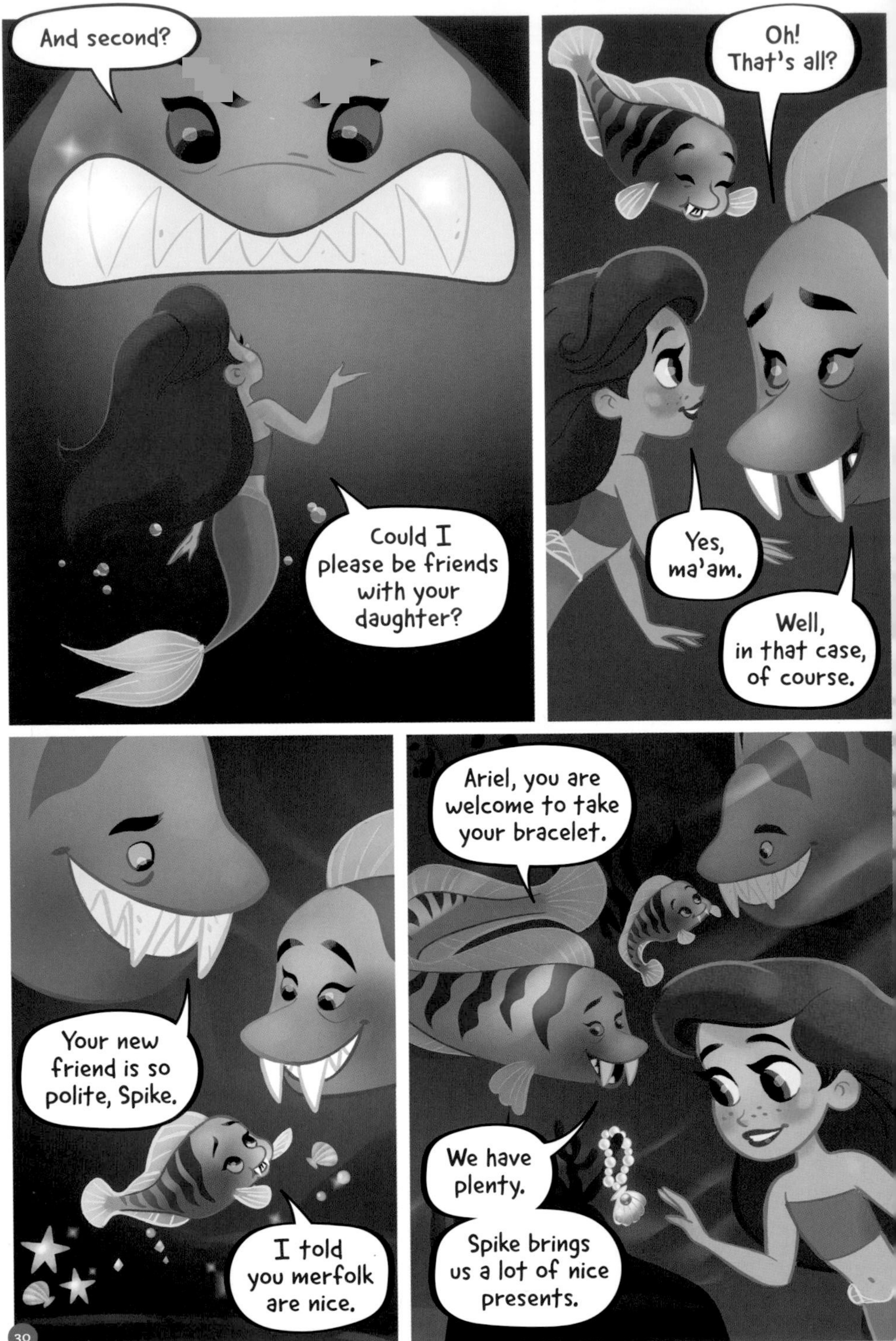
And second?
Could I please be friends with your daughter?
Oh! That's all?
Yes, ma'am.
Well, in that case, of course.
Your new friend is so polite, Spike.
I told you merfolk are nice.
Ariel, you are welcome to take your bracelet.
We have plenty.
Spike brings us a lot of nice presents.

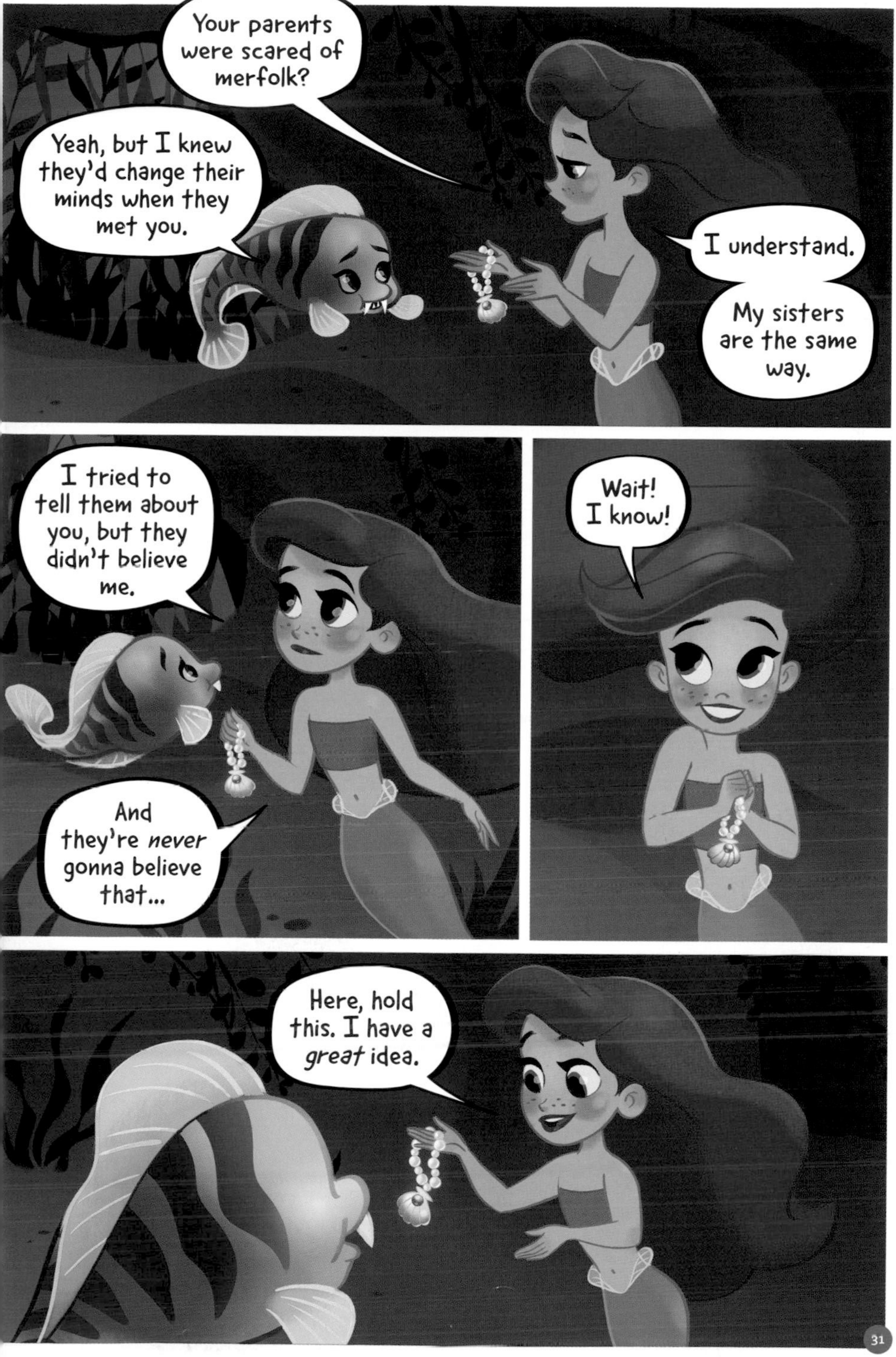
Your parents were scared of merfolk?
Yeah, but I knew they'd change their minds when they met you.
I understand.
My sisters are the same way.
I tried to tell them about you, but they didn't believe me.
And they're *never* gonna believe that...
Wait! I know!
Here, hold this. I have a *great* idea.

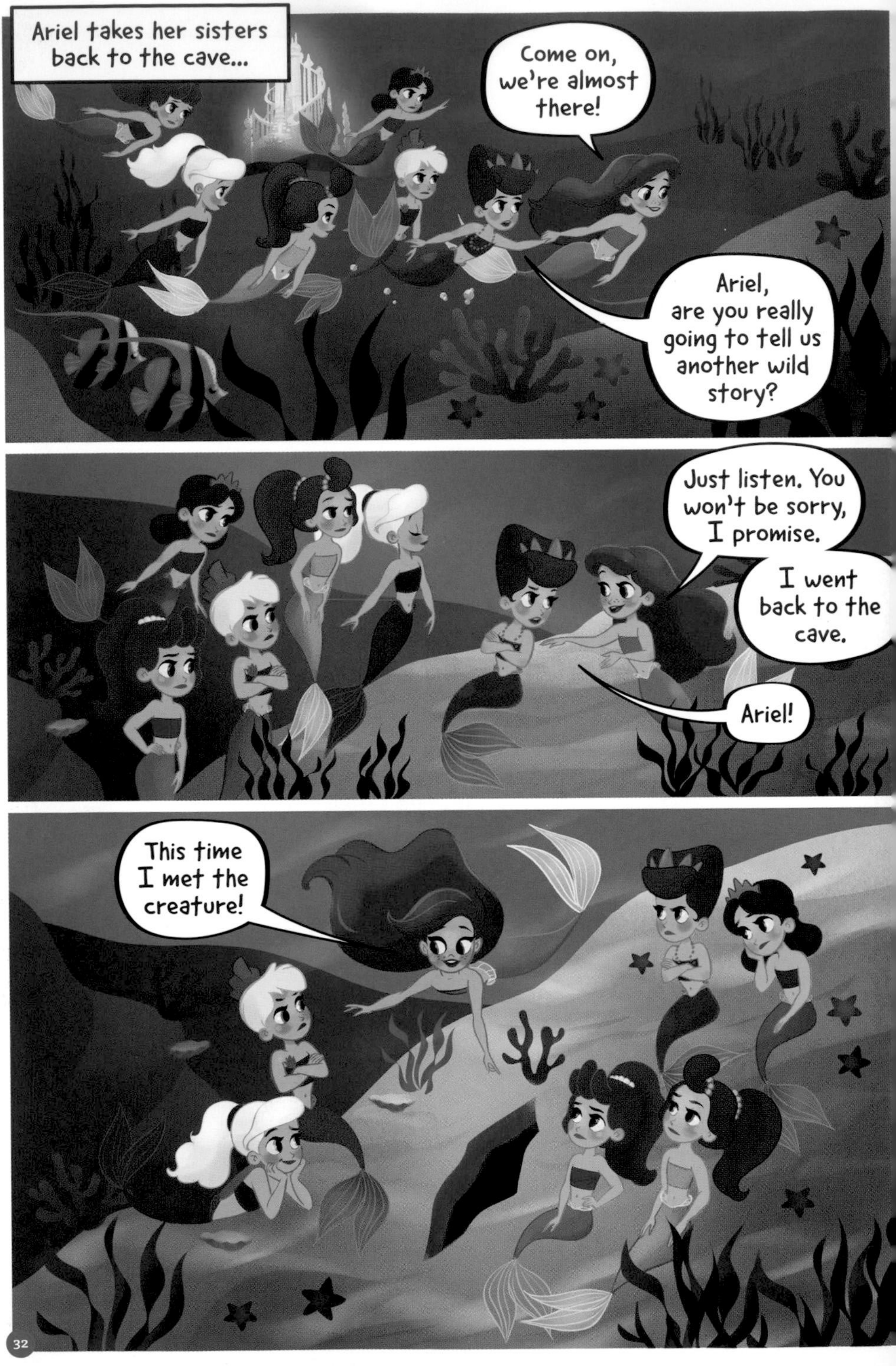
Ariel takes her sisters back to the cave...
Come on, we're almost there!
Ariel, are you really going to tell us another wild story?
Just listen. You won't be sorry, I promise.
I went back to the cave.
Ariel!
This time I met the creature!

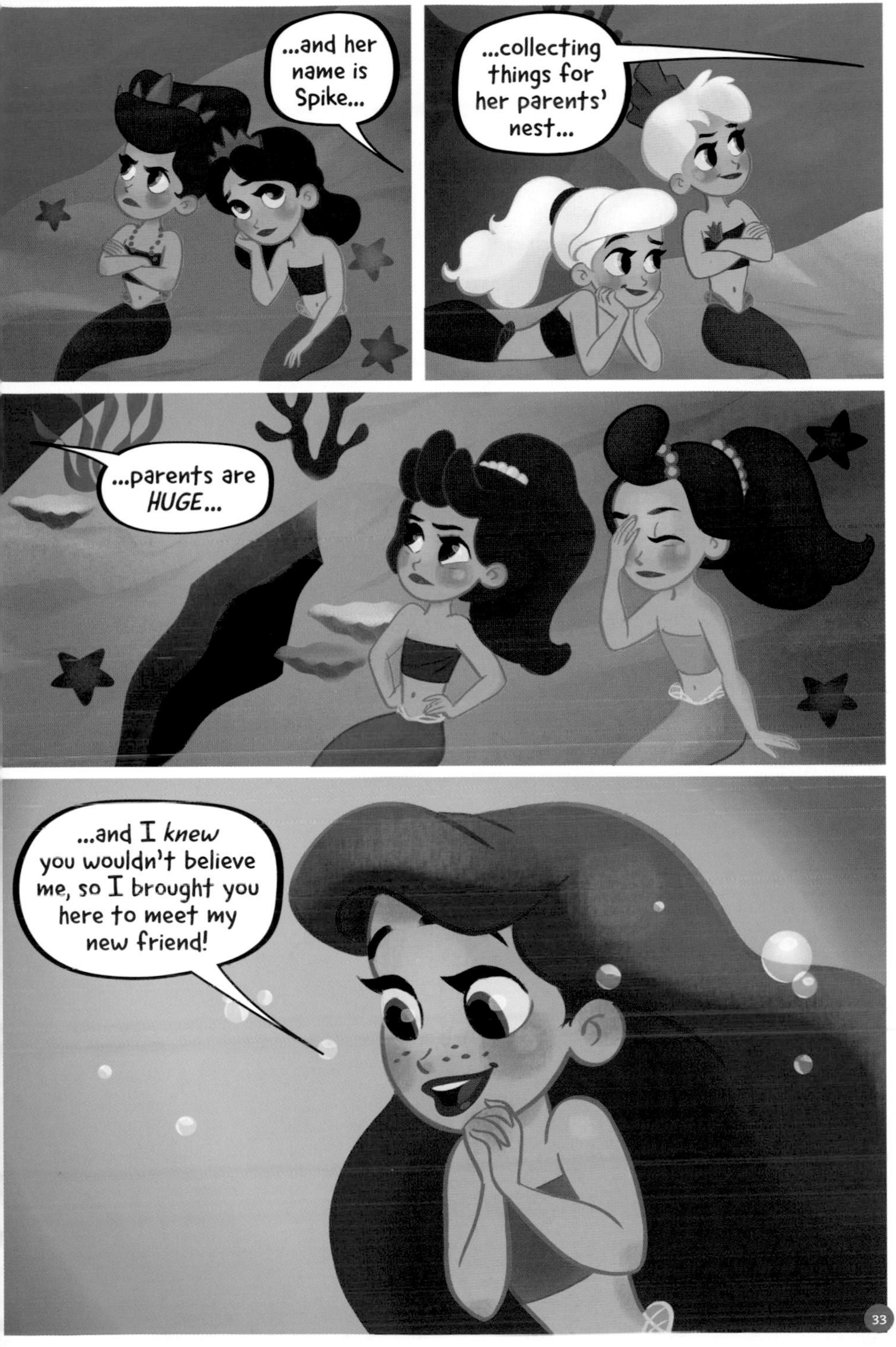
...and her name is Spike...
...collecting things for her parents' nest...
...parents are *HUGE*...
...and I *knew* you wouldn't believe me, so I brought you here to meet my new friend!

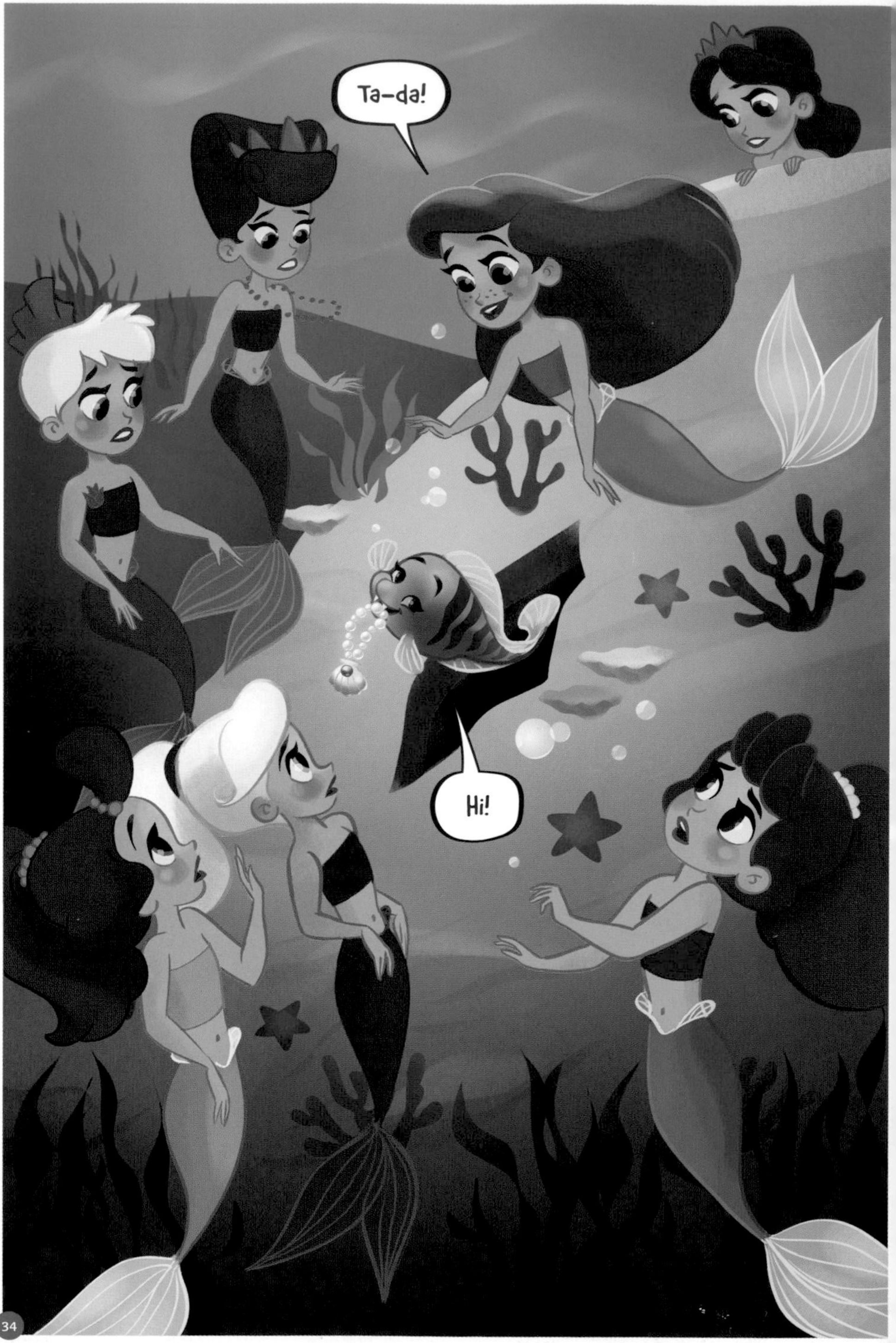
Ta-da!
Hi!

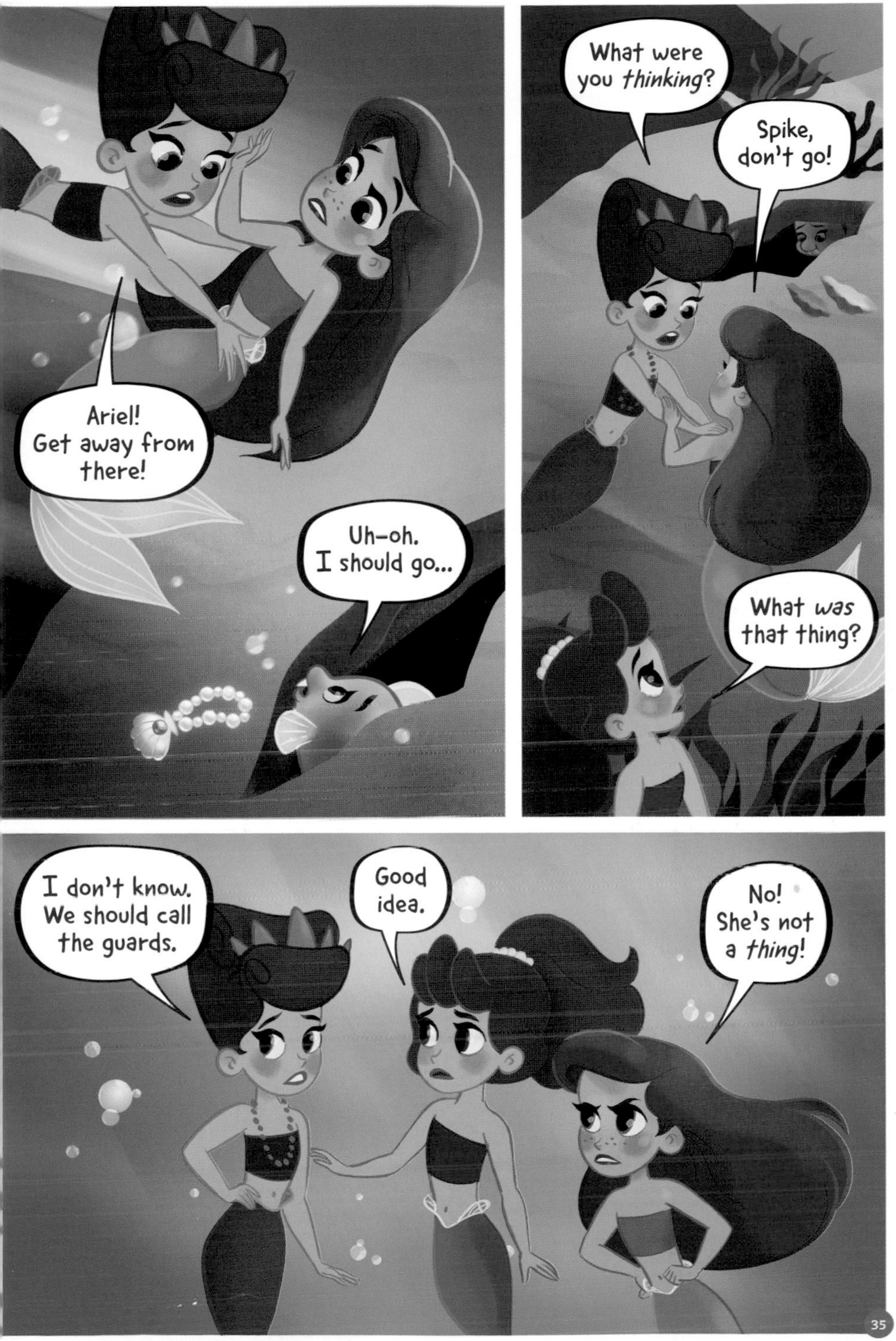
Ariel! Get away from there!
Uh-oh. I should go...
What were you *thinking*?
Spike, don't go!
What *was* that thing?
I don't know. We should call the guards.
Good idea.
No! She's not a *thing*!

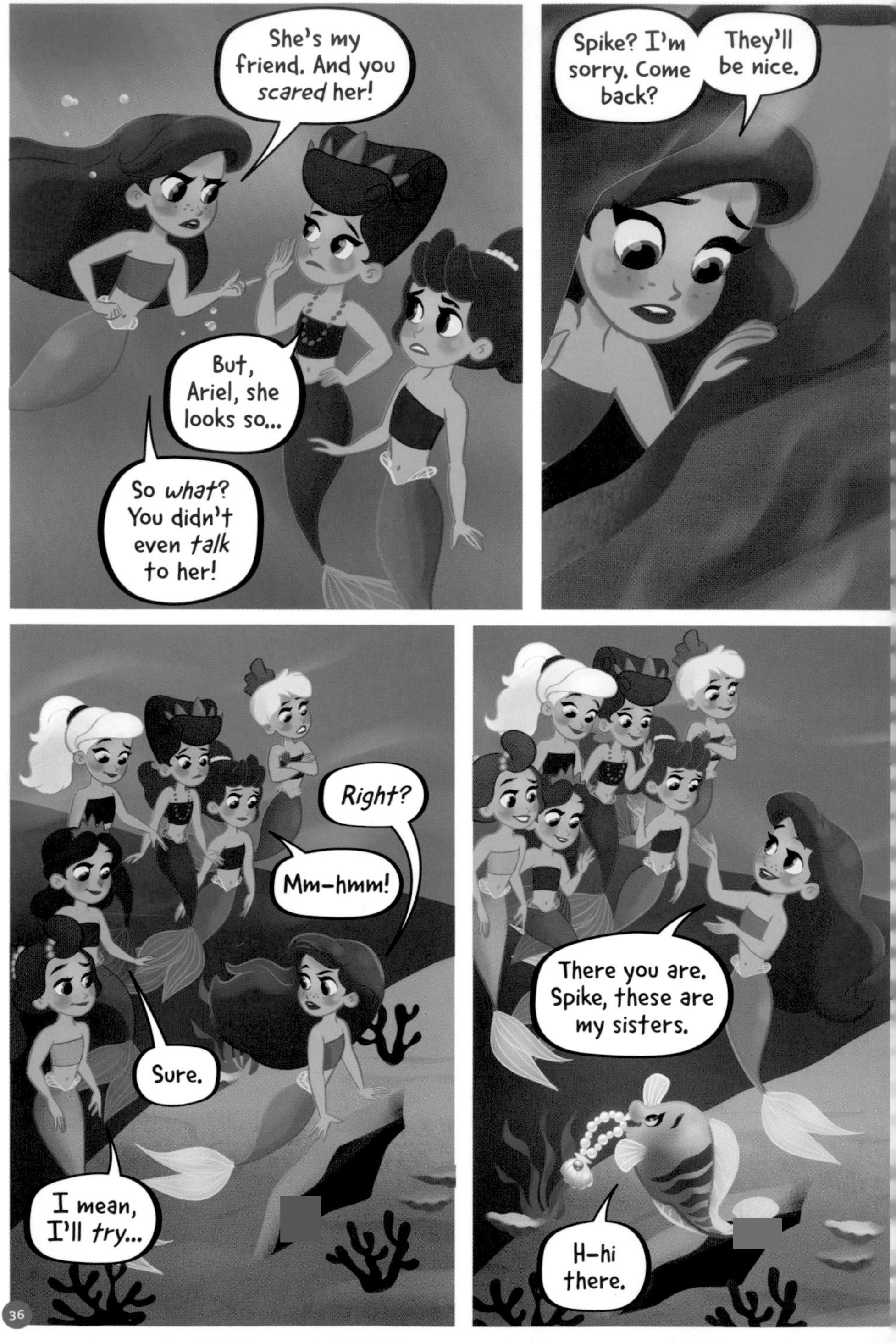
She's my friend. And you *scared* her!
But, Ariel, she looks so...
So *what*? You didn't even *talk* to her!
Spike? I'm sorry. Come back?
They'll be nice.
Right?
Mm-hmm!
Sure.
I mean, I'll *try*...
There you are. Spike, these are my sisters.
H-hi there.

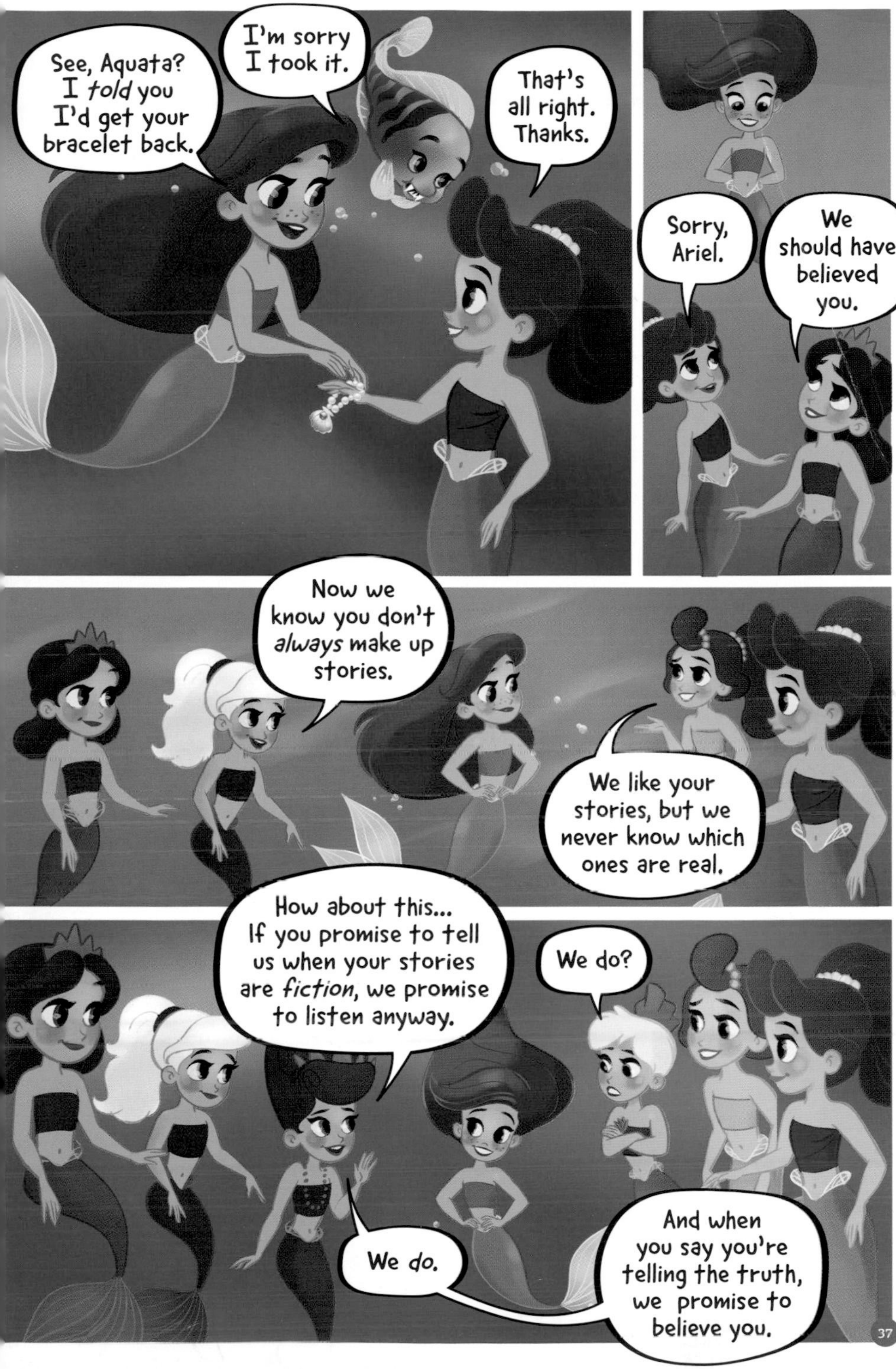
See, Aquata? I *told* you I'd get your bracelet back.
I'm sorry I took it.
That's all right. Thanks.
Sorry, Ariel.
We should have believed you.
Now we know you don't *always* make up stories.
We like your stories, but we never know which ones are real.
How about this... If you promise to tell us when your stories are *fiction*, we promise to listen anyway.
We do?
We *do*.
And when you say you're telling the truth, we promise to believe you.

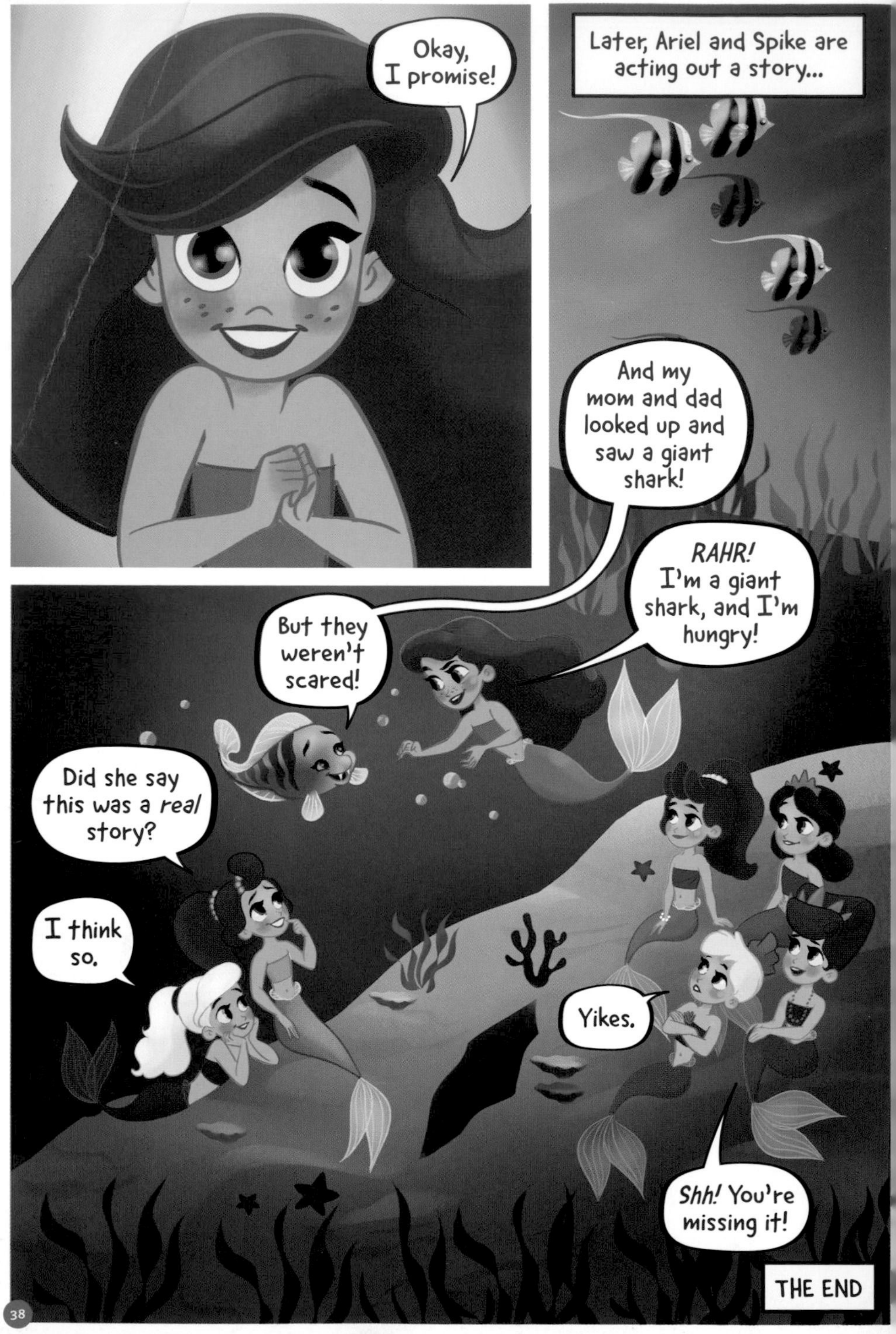

Okay, I promise!
Later, Ariel and Spike are acting out a story...
And my mom and dad looked up and saw a giant shark!
RAHR! I'm a giant shark, and I'm hungry!
But they weren't scared!
Did she say this was a *real* story?
I think so.
Yikes.
Shh! You're missing it!
THE END

A Trove of Out-of-this-World Activities!

What Happens Next?

Ariel and Spike have now become the best of friends—but in this story, we only hear about the beginning of their friendship. Can you think of some more adventures Ariel, her sisters, and Spike go on next? Do they explore deeper into the caves? Or do they search for treasure on sunken ships? The possibilities are as vast as the sea! What will you think of?

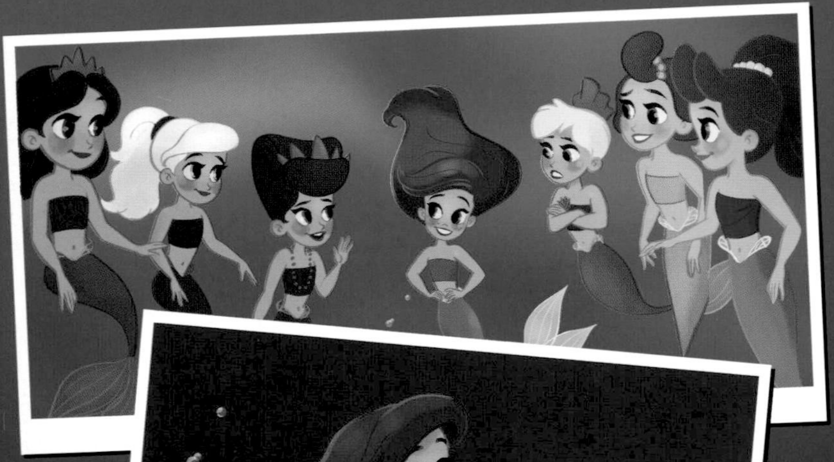

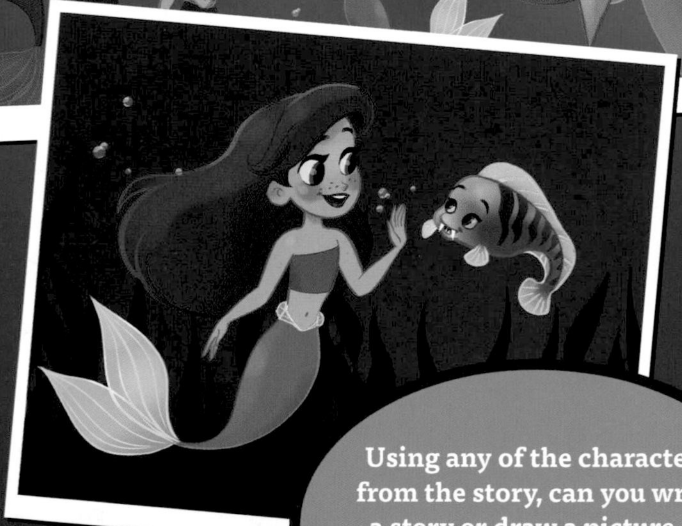

Using any of the characters from the story, can you write a story or draw a picture of what might happen next under the sea?

Scavenger Hunt!

Ariel and her sisters experienced a lot in this story—excitement, fear, and joy! But sometimes it's the little things that we often forget. Can you find these pictures of Ariel, her sisters, and Spike?

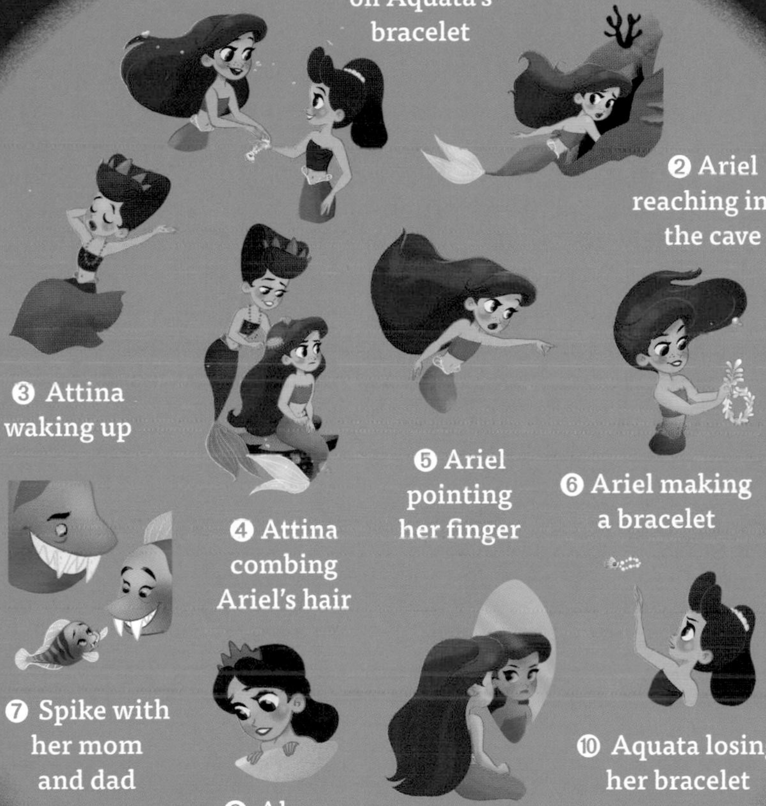

1. Ariel putting on Aquata's bracelet
2. Ariel reaching into the cave
3. Attina waking up
4. Attina combing Ariel's hair
5. Ariel pointing her finger
6. Ariel making a bracelet
7. Spike with her mom and dad
8. Alana behind the rock cave
9. Ariel looking at her reflection
10. Aquata losing her bracelet

Scavenger Hunt answer key:
1) Ariel putting the bracelet on Aquata, page 37; 2) Ariel reaching into the cave, page 9; 3)Attina waking up, page 15; 4) Attina combing Ariel's hair, page 16; 5) Ariel pointing her finger, page 7; 6) Ariel making a bracelet, page 19; 7) Spike with her mom and dad, page 30; 8) Alana hiding behind the rock cave, page 34; 9) Ariel looking at her reflection, page 16; 10) Aquata losing her bracelet, page 8

What Sea Animal Am I?

For this activity, you'll need a partner!

Imagine yourself as a sea animal. Maybe you're a fish, a clam, or a whale! The ocean is deep and expansive, so there are many animals to choose from! Once you've picked your animal, keep it a secret from your partner! They are going to try to guess what kind of animal you are!

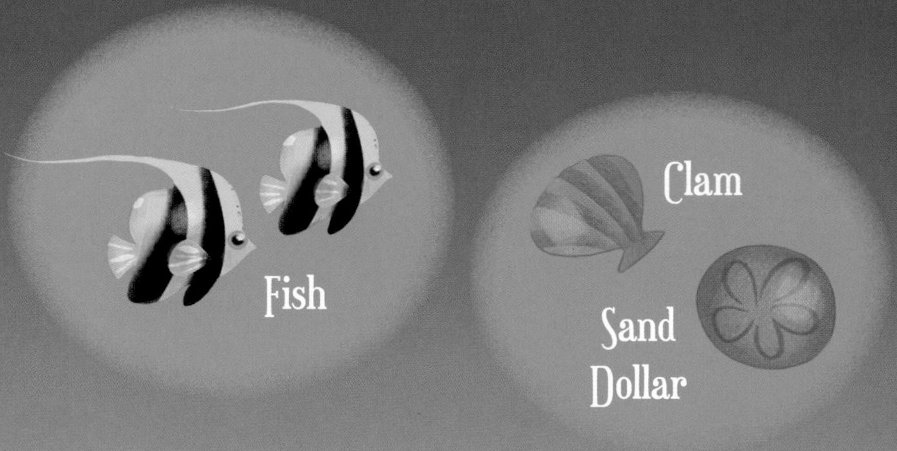

Fish
Clam
Sand Dollar

Once you've picked your sea animal, your partner can start asking you questions about yourself, until they can guess what animal you are. But, here's the hard part: you can only answer questions with "yes," "no," or "I don't know."

Below are a few examples of questions your partner might ask you!

- **Do you have a shell?**
- **Do you have fins?**
- **Do you eat plankton?**

Once your partner has successfully guessed what you are, swap roles! Have your partner imagine they are a type of aquatic animal and give *you* some hints!

Make an Acrostic Poem!

What exactly *is* an acrostic poem? This type of poem uses each of the letters in a topic word to begin each line of a poem. The lines of this poem can be sentences, or phases, or single words—but each line must describe or relate to the topic word.

Now that you know a little about acrostic poems, let's create some! You can try it here (or on a separate piece of paper) using the names of the characters from the story as topic words!

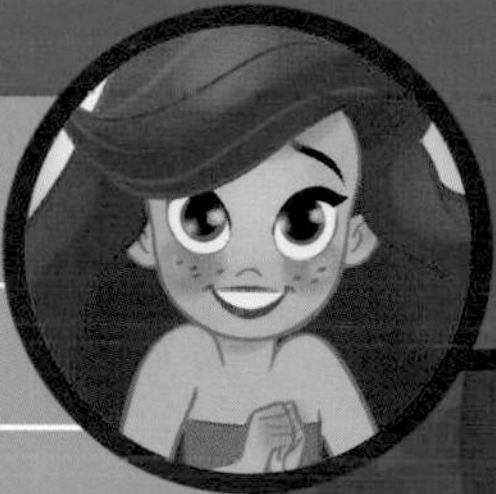

A ______________________

R ______________________

I ______________________

E ______________________

L ______________________

Using each letter in Ariel's name, think of one word that starts with that letter that could describe her.

Ariel has six older sisters: Aquata, Andrina, Arista, Attina, Adella, and Alana. With so many sisters, they can sometimes be difficult to tell apart. Try creating an acrostic poem for each of the sisters' names.

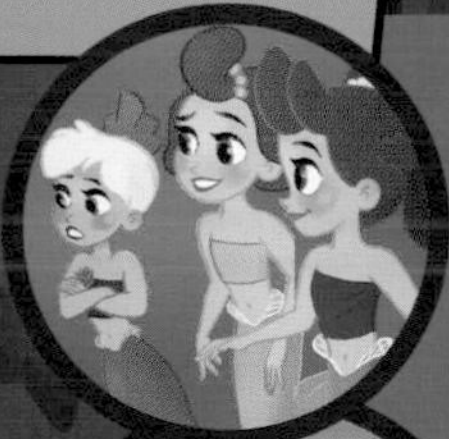

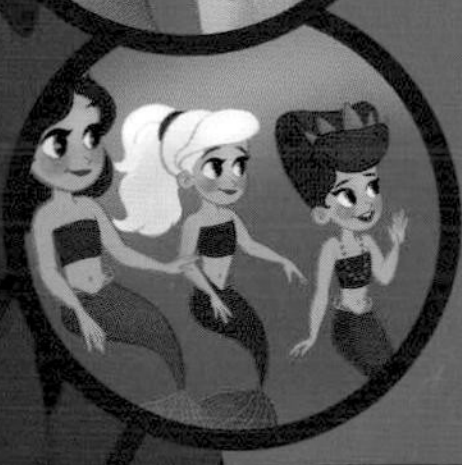

Turning these names into acrostic poems gives them a lot more meaning! What other names could you try this game with? Perhaps try it with *your own* name?

What's Missing from the Picture?

Look at the two pictures on these pages of Ariel and her sisters under the sea. It's the same picture . . . or is it? Can you spot 10 differences between picture A, and picture B? There are some things missing!

A

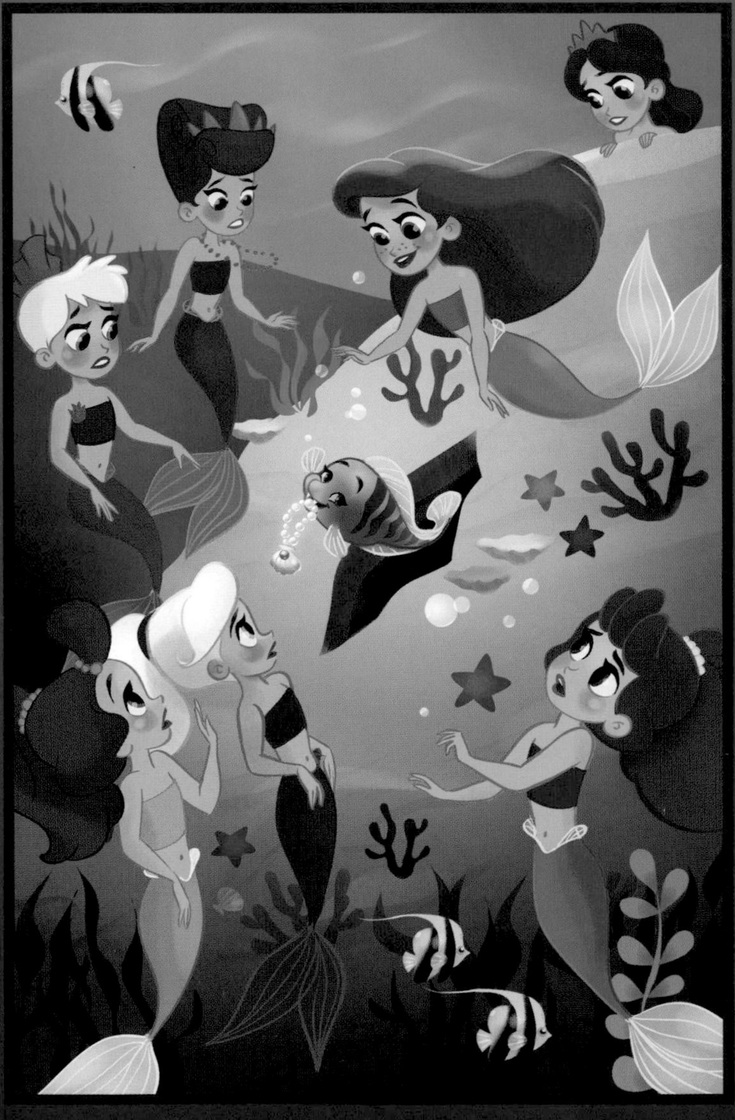

When you think you've found all the differences you can check your answers at the bottom of page 46!

B

Tell Me a Story . . .

Ariel loves to tell stories and now it's your turn!

Choose one character, one object, one event, and one location from the four boxes below. Then with all those chosen items, write or draw a story!

Pick a location

- ★ in a cave
- ★ in the ocean
- ★ on the shore
- ★ in a castle

Pick a Character(s)

- ★ Ariel
- ★ Spike
- ★ Spike's mom and dad
- ★ one of Ariel's sisters

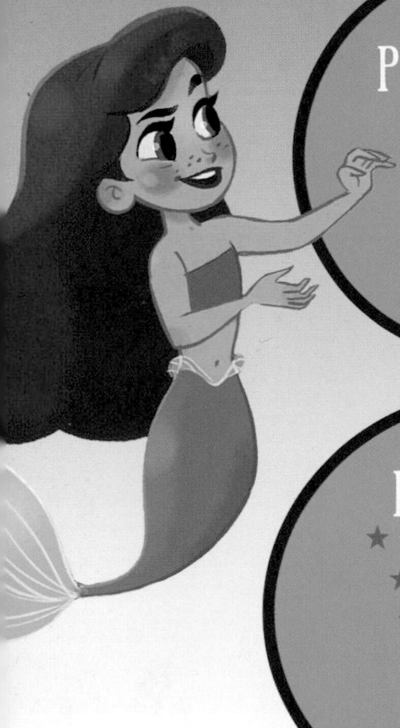

Pick an Object

- ★ seaweed
- ★ a boat
- ★ a shell
- ★ a piece of jewelry

Once you've created one story, make another one—try choosing a different character. Or, imagine yourself as the character and make the story from your perspective!

Pick an event

- ★ a family party
- ★ a discovery
- ★ encounter a dangerous creature
- ★ lost a trinket

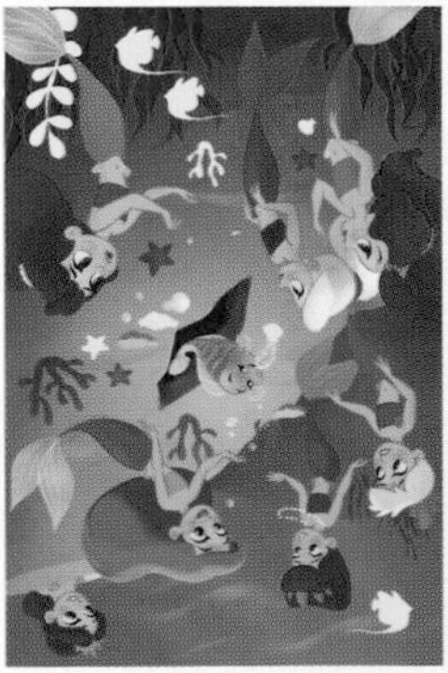

What's Missing from the Picture answer key:

DARK HORSE BOOKS

president and publisher Mike Richardson • collection editor Freddye Miller
collection assistant editor Judy Khuu • collection designer Anita Magaña
digital art technicians Christianne Gillenardo-Goudreau and Samantha Hummer

Neil Hankerson Executive Vice President • Tom Weddle Chief Financial Officer • Randy Stradley Vice President of Publishing • Nick McWhorter Chief Business Development Officer • Dale LaFountain Chief Information Officer • Matt Parkinson Vice President of Marketing • Cara Niece Vice President of Production and Scheduling • Mark Bernardi Vice President of Book Trade and Digital Sales • Ken Lizzi General Counsel • Dave Marshall Editor in Chief • Davey Estrada Editorial Director • Chris Warner Senior Books Editor • Cary Grazzini Director of Specialty Projects • Lia Ribacchi Art Director • Vanessa Todd-Holmes Director of Print Purchasing • Matt Dryer Director of Digital Art and Prepress • Michael Gombos Senior Director of Licensed Publications • Kari Yadro Director of Custom Programs

DISNEY PUBLISHING WORLDWIDE GLOBAL MAGAZINES, COMICS AND PARTWORKS

PUBLISHER Lynn Waggoner • EDITORIAL TEAM Bianca Coletti (Director, Magazines), Guido Frazzini (Director, Comics), Carlotta Quattrocolo (Executive Editor), Stefano Ambrosio (Executive Editor, New IP), Camilla Vedove (Senior Manager, Editorial Development), Behnoosh Khalili (Senior Editor), Julie Dorris (Senior Editor), Mina Riazi (Assistant Editor), Jonathan Manning (Assistant Editor) • DESIGN Enrico Soave (Senior Designer) • ART Ken Shue (VP, Global Art), Manny Mederos (Senior Illustration Manager, Comics and Magazines), Roberto Santillo (Creative Director), Marco Ghiglione (Creative Manager), Stefano Attardi (Computer Art Designer) • PORTFOLIO MANAGEMENT Olivia Ciancarelli (Director) • BUSINESS & MARKETING Mariantonietta Galla (Marketing Manager), Virpi Korhonen (Editorial Manager)

Disney Princess: Ariel and the Sea Wolf

Published by Dark Horse Books
A division of Dark Horse Comics LLC
10956 SE Main Street
Milwaukie, OR 97222

DarkHorse.com

To find a comics shop in your area, visit comicshoplocator.com

First edition: April 2019
ISBN 978-1-50671-203-1
Digital ISBN 978-1-50671-204-8

1 3 5 7 9 10 8 6 4 2
Printed in China

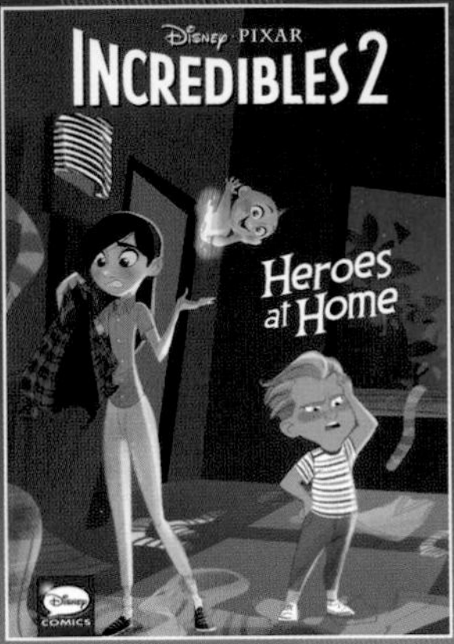
Disney·PIXAR
INCREDIBLES 2
Heroes at Home
Disney COMICS

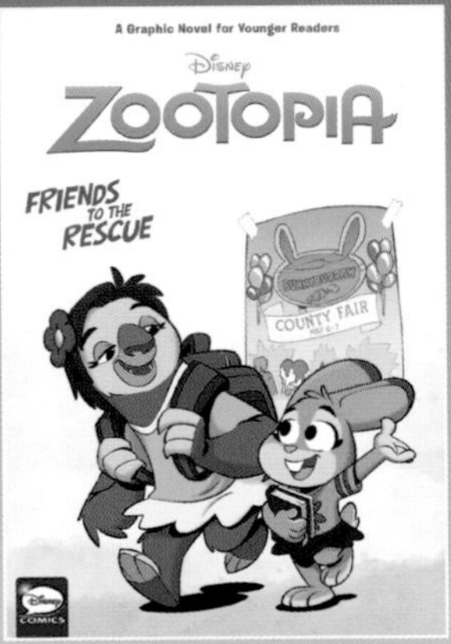
A Graphic Novel for Younger Readers
Disney
ZOOTOPIA
FRIENDS TO THE RESCUE
COUNTY FAIR
Disney COMICS

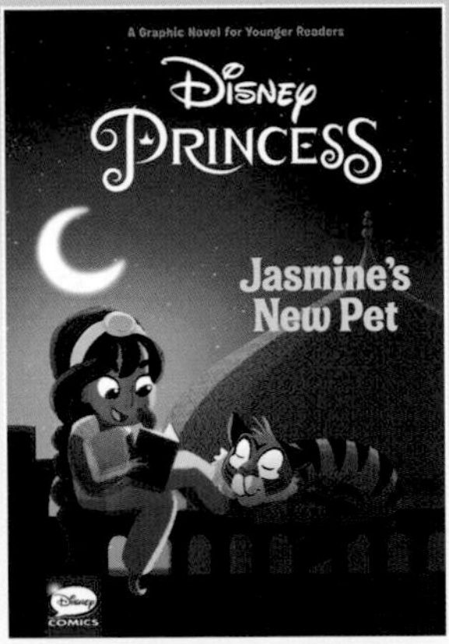
A Graphic Novel for Younger Readers
Disney
PRINCESS
Jasmine's New Pet
Disney COMICS

LOOKING FOR BOOKS FOR YOUNGER READERS?

$7.99 each!

EACH VOLUME INCLUDES A SECTION OF FUN ACTIVITIES!

DISNEY·PIXAR INCREDIBLES 2: HEROES AT HOME

Violet and Dash are part of a Super family, and they are trying to help out at home. Can they pick up groceries and secretly stop some bad guys? And then can they clean up the house while Jack-Jack is "sleeping"?

ISBN 978-1-50670-943-7 | $7.99

DISNEY ZOOTOPIA: FRIENDS TO THE RESCUE

Young Judy Hopps proves she's a brave little bunny when she helps a classmate. And can a quick-thinking young Nick Wilde liven up a birthday party? Friends save the day in these tales of Zootopia!

ISBN 978-1-50671-054-9 | $7.99

DISNEY PRINCESS: JASMINE'S NEW PET

Jasmine has a new pet tiger, Rajah, but he's not quite ready for palace life. Will she be able to train the young cub before the Sultan finds him another home?

ISBN 978-1-50671-052-5 | $7.99

AVAILABLE AT YOUR LOCAL COMICS SHOP OR BOOKSTORE! TO FIND A COMICS SHOP IN YOUR AREA, VISIT COMICSHOPLOCATOR.COM

DARK HORSE BOOKS

For more information or to order direct: On the web: DarkHorse.com | Email: mailorder@darkhorse.com | Phone: 1-800-862-0052 Mon.–Fri. 9 a.m. to 5 p.m. Pacific Time

Disney COMICS